Embracing Desire

By Marie Tuhart

https://www.marietuhart.com/

intelligence technologies to generate text without Author's specific and express permission.

QUALITY CONTROL: We strive to produce error-free books, but even with all the eyes that see the story during the production process, slips get by. So please, if you find a typo or any formatting issues, please let us know at **marie@marietuhart.com** so that we may correct it.

Thank you!

Embracing Desire

Three hearts reunited, entangled in passion

Katie Crane decides it's time to confront her past and the desires that drove her away from home. Eight years ago, she fled from the two men she loved because she feared they would destroy her. Now back home with a newfound understanding of the lifestyle, she questions her strength to embrace her own submission.

Katie's unexpected return is both exhilarating and nerve-wracking for Ry McKade and Jed Malloy. Forced to confront their own insecurities, they'll have to choose to let Katie in again. Letting her in means risking their hearts all over again, and if she leaves again there could be irrevocable damage.

As the three of them navigate their new relationship, tensions mount and emotions run high. Katie's return could mark the beginning of everything they've yearned for, or the end of the only family they've ever known.

ACKNOWLEGMENTS

Laurie, thank you for all your support.

Red Quill Editing team, this story has always been one I've wanted to tell. You helped me see what I was missing and things that needed to be fleshed out. Thank you for all the phone calls and doing such a great job.

Publisher's Note: This books contains adult situations. MMF, sexy situations, discussion of past trauma's, past physical abuse (not to main characters), dominant males. No Artificial Intelligence was used in the writing of this book.

To My Readers:

This book contains elements of the BDSM lifestyle that are only true in this book. There are various relationship dynamics in the lifestyle, which are decided between the people involved. While I have researched and talked with people in the lifestyle, this is my take on how my characters choose to live.

If you decide to explore the lifestyle yourself, please remember to always be safe. Never go home with someone you don't know. Attend a munch or a smaller get-together first to see if this is something you want in your life. Reading and living are very different.

Enjoy.

Chapter 1

"This stops now, Walter." Katie Crane's hands tightened on the steering wheel. "I'm not coming back to New York City. No matter what you or my father want." Lord why hadn't she blocked Walter's number? Maybe out of guilt for leaving abruptly, but what did Walter expect? The man was a hypocrite like her father.

"Quit being a bitch and listen to reason."

Katie saw red. She wasn't the villain in this. "You're a bastard." She yanked off the Bluetooth earpiece and tossed it out the window of the moving car. If only it was that easy to get rid of her ex and her father, life would be grand, and she wouldn't have run away eight years ago with her father when he promised her the world.

Now she was going home to Felton's Creek Washington. Warmth spread through her. She'd already talked with her grandmother who, bless her, never held it against her for leaving when her father arrived shortly after her eighteenth birthday.

Katie sighed. She'd thought she could finally have a relationship with her father, but it wasn't to be. It was a shame it took her so long to realize it. And what about… She shook her head.

She was coming home for more than the two men she abandoned. This was for her. She missed the simpler life of Felton's Creek. New York City was always bustling, and because she worked for her father's firm, full of business dinners and parties. She shivered. No more.

Her mind turned to Ry and Jed. How would they react to her coming back? Gran had told her they were angry when she left but accepted it. She hoped so or this homecoming was going to be very uncomfortable.

She bit her lip. Maybe this wasn't such a good idea. What if Ry and Jed didn't want anything to do with her? Could she live with that?

After the past few years, yes, she could. She was tired of playing it safe and listening to the wrong people. Her home town might be small, but she could handle seeing them. She'd made the right decision. It was time to go home to stay. She missed Gran, and while talking to her, she'd found out Ry and Jed didn't have anyone special in their lives.

Besides, after reporting her father to the government, he wasn't going to be asking her back or coming after her. Her stomach churned. Walter calling her didn't make sense.

A blinding blue light caught Katie's eye. Oh crap. A large SUV with lights flashing filled her rearview mirror. Glancing at the speedometer confirmed she wasn't speeding. The cruise control was engaged.

With a flick of her wrist, she turned her signal on and brought the car to a stop on the shoulder. Just what she needed, a ticket only ten miles from Felton's Creek. She'd never live this down.

Katie kept her hands on the wheel while watching the vehicle in her rearview mirror. A tall, muscular man climbed out of the SUV. She caught a glimpse of dark hair before it was hidden beneath his hat. The moment he stepped up to her door, she lowered the window.

"Good afternoon, officer." She was proud her voice

was steady after the way Walter had badgered her. Her gaze shifted to the officer's face. Oh my. His eyes were covered by reflective sunglasses, but those didn't detract from a straight nose, sculptured cheekbones, and a stubborn chin. All things she shouldn't be noticing right now.

"Good afternoon, ma'am." His smooth whiskey voice slid over her skin in a gentle caress. "May I see your driver's license, proof of insurance, and registration please?"

"Of course." Katie gathered the documents from the glove compartment and her purse and handed them to the officer. His hand touched hers, and Katie caught her breath.

There was something familiar about him. Something she couldn't put her finger on. When she left Felton's Creek at eighteen, Ry's father had been the sheriff. But that was before he'd passed away in an accident. Who was this new sheriff, and why was he familiar to her? She pushed her confusing thoughts away. No sense in muddying the waters.

"You drove all the way from New York City?" His tone held censure.

"I did." Her chin rose. She wasn't a child anymore. She was tired of men treating her like she was eighteen, a naïve eighteen at that. At twenty-six, she was a woman with her own mind and attitude. As her father found out when she left New York City five days ago. "Why did you pull me over, officer?"

He grinned as if she amused him. "Littering."

"Littering?" She'd never littered in her life.

"You threw your earpiece out the window, and it shattered on the road."

Katie's mouth dropped. He pulled her over because of her earpiece? She started to speak, but there was a screech, and his radio went off.

"Excuse me." Long, sensual fingers pressed the radio on his shoulder. "What's up, Betty?"

"There's a problem at the Red Dog. They're requesting your assistance."

"Tell them I'll be right there." He glanced at her license quickly and handed it and her other paperwork back. "Duty calls. Please drive carefully, and don't litter."

Katie took her documents and watched him in the mirror as he sauntered back to his vehicle and climbed in. A shiver of sensual excitement crawled up her spine. What was it about him? Something familiar, yet not. And damn if her heart wasn't pounding, her hands shaking with excitement, and her pussy twitched. Not so good.

The SUV pulled out and around her vehicle before disappearing down the road. Katie shook off the sensual haze, put her things away, and pulled back onto the road, headed for home. The word wrapped her in a sense of warmth and security.

She never thought she'd miss her tiny home town as much as she had. Eight years in New York City was enough. But she'd missed more than the town. She'd missed her gran. Gran would be thrilled she was home to stay. She wondered how Ry and Jed looked today. She bet they'd changed. How would they feel now that she'd come home to stay? Because it was to stay. Right where she belonged.

* * * *

Ryland McKade strode over to the outdoor ring to see Jed, his best friend and lover, working with one of the horses. What an interesting day it had been. Katie was back. He grinned. She hadn't recognized him when he pulled her over earlier. He was sort of surprised, but then not. It had been eight years, and he'd changed a lot in those years.

Katie had changed too. The second he realized it was her, his heart stuttered. Part of him wanted to ask her why she'd stayed away so long; another wanted to yell at her for leaving, and another wanted to drag her out of the car and kiss her until neither of them could breathe.

"Be with you in a second, Ry," Jed yelled, leading the horse to the barn.

Ry raised his hand to let Jed know he'd heard him. How would Jed feel about Katie being back? Katie's leaving had left Jed floundering for a while. He and Jed had become lovers after she'd left. How would she feel about that? Ry ran his hands through his dark hair. His stomach tumbled around, and his groin tightened.

Eight long years, and Katie looked almost the same. She'd cut her long, deep brown hair to her jawline, and he had to admit it looked good on her. Her green eyes had been filled with confusion when he'd pulled her over.

In their brief encounter, he noticed a confidence in her voice that hadn't been there before. How her breasts rose and fell beneath her shirt when she looked him over.

"Hey, Ry, you'll never guess who called me today." Jed strode out of the barn.

"Who?" He watched Jed amble over and rested his foot on the lower rung of the fence.

"Miss Mazie."

"Katie's gran? Is she okay?" It didn't matter that Katie had left him and Jed all those years ago, Miss Mazie was still part of their extended family.

"Miss Mazie, yes. Katie's coming home." Jed avoided

eye contact.

"I know." Ry placed his hand on Jed's forearm, feeling the muscles tighten.

"How the hell did you find out?" Jed's blue eyes widened.

The astonishment in Jed's voice made Ry laugh. "I pulled Katie over ten miles outside of town."

Jed frowned. "Katie was speeding?"

"Let's walk." Ry didn't want to discuss this where Jed's workers could overhear. They fell into step and strolled away from the barn, out toward the open pasture. "What did Miss Mazie say?"

"Just that Katie had called her, and she'd be home today." Jed pushed his hat back and rubbed his forehead. "Miss Mazie always liked us."

"Yeah." Ry stared out at the land without really seeing it. Katie was back, and his mind raced with the possibilities along with all the potential disasters. Was she back to stay and ready to accept their lifestyle? Or was this just a visit? Perhaps she was involved with someone, or she couldn't accept them as they were.

"How did she look?" Jed asked, his tone eager.

"Beautiful." Ry closed his eyes and pictured her again. "She cut her hair, but it suits her, and she's filled out. She's a woman now."

"What did she say to you?"

Ry opened his eyes and laughed. "She didn't recognize me."

Jed chuckled. "That is surprising." He sauntered over to the big oak tree and leaned against it. "What are we going to do?"

"I don't know." Katie had run right after her eighteenth birthday, two nights after he and Jed made love to her and explained what they wanted from her. They both wanted a relationship with her. A true committed poly relationship, along with some bondage and discipline.

"Miss Mazie invited us to a welcome home party for Katie tomorrow."

Ry's fingers clenched. Could he get involved with Katie again? Hell, who was he kidding? The woman still had him tied up in knots, and he didn't mind it at all. "I won't hide who I am from her, Jed."

He'd learned to control the anger he had at her abandonment of him and Jed and channeled it into learning more and more about being an excellent Dominant.

"I'm not asking you to." Jed placed a hand on Ry's shoulder, squeezing gently. "Maybe keep your über dominant side toned down a bit. You do tend to get a little overbearing."

"She ran, Jed. I'm not sure I can handle her running again."

"I understand. Katie leaving eight years ago hurt us both. But we did kind of spring the type of relationship we wanted on her."

"What was I supposed to do?" Ry stepped away from Jed and kicked at the tree roots. "I'm a Dominant."

"At that time, we only knew what our parents had taught us." Jed ran his palms over his thighs. "But we were both too young to take on a relationship like that. I was twenty-one and you twenty-two."

"I knew what I wanted." Ry stared at Jed.

"You knew what you thought you wanted." Jed shook his head. "The poly dynamic is a lot more than what our parents knew or had."

Ry wanted to argue, but Jed was right. "Katie is a submissive; that I'm sure of."

"I feel that as well, but I'm a switch. She needs to understand our relationship, and how she fits into it."

"Yeah."

"We can't rush things, this time." Jed placed his hand on Ry's forearm.

"I know." He sighed. "I'm worried."

"About what?"

"What happened after she left." Ry had been upset, more so than anyone thought. He'd taken his motorcycle and ridden it into Seattle and went to a BDSM club. One his father had told him to stay away from. It wasn't until he saw a sadistic Dominant scene with a submissive. The man had left welts on the submissive's body even after she safeworded and before anyone could stop him.

A part of Ry wanted to do that to a submissive, to whip out his anger. Luckily, he'd pulled himself back and walked out of the club. The image of the submissive stayed with him for years while he dealt with his anger. "I don't want to hurt, Katie."

"You lost control once, Ry. Once. And even then, you didn't injure anyone but yourself. You would never hurt Katie, just like you would never hurt me." Jed took Ry's hand and placed it on his chest. "I'm more worried if Katie will accept the relationship between us."

"Shit." Not only did they have the past to deal with, but also the present and future. In all his dreams, he never thought it would be this hard or this frightening. "We have to show her it's all about love and desire."

"Not only for each other but for her as well." Jed stepped closer to Ry. "She didn't mind us each making love to her that night, and she's always been receptive to a threesome with us. We were the ones who waited until she was eighteen."

"Legal age." Ry's free hand crept around Jed's neck. "I don't think I'd be able to let her go this time."

"Let's hope we don't have to."

"We need a plan for tomorrow. She'll need time. He tugged Jed closer. The scent of leather and horse helped to calm Ry's nerves.

"Plan tonight," Jed whispered before capturing Ry's lips.

Katie was home, and Jed was in his arms. He would make this work.

Chapter 2

The next day, Katie slipped through the doorway, and into her grandmother's kitchen, away from her welcome home party. She needed a few minutes to gather her wild emotions after the two men had walked into the house several minutes ago. Ryland McKade and Jedidiah Malloy.

Standing at the sink, she stared out the window. Welcome back to Felton's Creek. Her heart jumped. She'd run from Ry and Jed eight years ago, afraid of her own sexuality. Now, she was more secure with herself, but what about them? She was putting horse before the cart. They needed to talk first.

From the second she saw them enter the house, Ry and Jed had dominated her thoughts, made her pussy wet, and caused the blood to heat in her veins. Only these two could do that by just walking into her space.

Now she was wishing and praying she'd done the right thing in coming back home. She knew what type of relationship Ry and Jed wanted. They'd made it clear when she was eighteen, and from chatting with her grandmother, it didn't sound like anything had changed.

Why hadn't she'd talked to them before coming back? Maybe because she'd been afraid. Afraid of her own wants and needs. But she had to try. She'd regret it the rest of her life if she didn't give them the chance. The air in the kitchen changed, and she opened her eyes. It was just dark enough outside she could see their reflections in the glass.

Her heart pounded.

Ry and Jed sauntered through the door and over to her. Her breath caught in her throat. Ry was still taller than Jed and had filled out in the past years. His features were more serious than she remembered, but there was something else, something… Oh hell, he was the cop who had pulled her over yesterday.

Jed. She turned her attention to him. He was still taller than her by a couple of inches, his skin tan from the sun, with laugh lines around his blue eyes. His brown hair brushed his collar. He'd filled out over the years, but was still smaller than Ry.

Little sparks of nervous energy caused her hands to twitch. She shifted from one foot to the other. No time like the present. She would have to deal with them on a daily basis.

"Hi, guys," she said, smiling at their reflections in the glass as her stomach clenched.

"Katie." Ry's rich voice sent a shiver of awareness up her spine.

"Kitty Kat." Jed's soft-as-butter voice caused her heart to speed up.

Katie took a deep breath and turned only to run into a hard chest. Lifting her head, she gazed into Ry's eyes. His firm hands framed her waist, guiding her away from the sink until Jed was able to step behind her.

Oh, crap. Her heart fluttered and excitement filled her bones. They were not going slow this time. Jed's chest brushed against her back, his hands settling right above Ry's on her waist. Pure molten heat flooded her pussy. She was stuck between two hard bodies, and neither her mind nor her heart was protesting.

Ry nodded. The two men guided her across the room,

where Ry reached back and opened the pantry door. Once they were inside, the click of the lock vibrated in her ears.

Why wasn't she protesting? Because she didn't want to. The three of them were alone in the small room. Her mouth went dry as the small light flickered to life. Enough light to see things, but not the harshness of the overhead light bulb.

"Welcome home." Jed's breath skimmed her neck before his lips touched her skin.

"It's been too damn long." Ry didn't hesitate, his mouth closing over hers.

Her heart pounded as Ry's mouth devoured hers. Jed nipped at her skin with little bites where her neck and shoulder met, and she gasped.

Two sets of hands roamed over her body. Ry cupped her ass, pulling her against his hard cock. Jed teased the underside of her breasts, making her nipples pebble while he pressed his equally hard erection against her ass.

"My turn." The words barely registered before Ry released her lips. Strong fingers cupped her chin, her head turned, and Jed took her mouth. His lips were softer, but his kiss was as hard and demanding as Ry's, just less urgent.

Her brain grappled with the way they tasted. Ry, metal and coffee. Jed, mint and the outdoors. Oh, God. They tasted the same as they had when she was eighteen.

Her body was melting between them. She curled one arm around Jed's neck, and the other hand began caressing Ry's chest. Her helplessness to resist these two men was starting again. And did she care? At the moment, no, but she'd come home knowing they weren't going to play it safe.

A thump against the wall caused Katie to jump, but it

also helped clear her head of the sensual web the men had spun over her. They were in her grandmother's pantry, her grandmother's house, making out like a bunch of teenagers. This had to stop. Now. Ground rules needed to be put in place.

"Guys," she whispered after pulling her mouth free from Jed's and catching her breath.

Lips caressed each side of her neck, hands roaming over her body, making her squirm. But when skin met skin, she had to stop this before they ripped off their clothes. And she knew of only one way to make them stop.

"Red."

Their heads snapped up, and their hands stilled.

"What did you just say?" Ry stared down at her, his gray eyes flat and cold.

"Red." An icy shiver slithered up her spine, but she held her ground.

Jed swore softly, removed his hands, and took a step back. Ry kept staring at her, but he, too, released her and pulled away.

Katie took a deep breath and let it out. It helped calm her racing heart, but their scent filled her nostrils instead. Sandalwood for Ry and leather for Jed, and those scents had haunted her every night. It wasn't fair they could tie her up in knots so quickly, but then she knew what she was getting into by coming home. She feared she couldn't handle them or what they wanted.

"This is my grandmother's house. We will not do this here." She had to be strong if she was going to enter a relationship with these two men. It had to be on terms she could live with, or they could destroy her heart.

Ry cleared his throat. "How did you know the word red would stop us?"

Bracing her back against one of the shelves, she stared at the two men in front of her. "I'm no longer the shy, naïve eighteen-year-old you once knew." And she wasn't. Thanks to some of the friends she'd made in New York, she'd learned a lot about the world they described to her. Their world.

"I see." Ry rubbed his chin, evaluating her with an intense gaze, as if he was assessing a flight risk.

She wasn't going to run this time. She wouldn't leave Felton's Creek; she'd had enough of the big city and chasing a dream that wasn't possible. She wouldn't go back to her father's machinations. She thrust her failure away. This was not the time or the place.

"You do realize what you're saying?" Jed asked.

"I hope so," she whispered as doubt crept into her mind. Could she handle them? She almost laughed out loud. Handle wasn't the right word. No one could *handle* them. They were their own men.

"Then let the games begin," Jed said.

They started toward her, and Katie threw her hands up. "Nope. There are things we need to discuss, and you two need to back off."

Both men stood like statues.

She had to hold back a nervous giggle at the surprised and hungry look on their faces. Her body trembled, but she had to do this. It was difficult for her to deny them, but she had to. Her rules. "This is my grandmother's house. I will not do this here. There is no discussion around it. It's a hard limit."

"Who the fuck taught you?" Ry took a step forward.

"Ry." Jed grabbed his arm. "Katie is right. This isn't the time or place."

Jed's hard stare made Katie shiver. Okay, so maybe

Jed wasn't as easygoing as she remembered.

"Tomorrow night. Our house. Seven." Ry ground the words out.

Katie nodded. At least they were taking her seriously. She squeezed past them to the door of the pantry. Her skin felt singed from the contact.

"And if you're late, you will be punished," Jed said as her hand curved around the knob.

She froze, her heart doing triple time. "Punished? No. We haven't covered all the bases yet, and until we do, don't overstep. And I'm always on time when I make a commitment."

She slipped out and closed the door behind her, resting her back against the solid wood. Oh. Dear. God. She was going into the lion's den.

* * * *

Ry stared at the pantry door, willing the acute hurt rolling through his veins to subside. "I want to know who taught her." His voice vibrated.

"We'll find out, and you need to calm down, Ry." Jed's calm tone wasn't helping Ry control the beast inside him.

"Someone else taught her, Jed. Not us. It should have been us." Ry ground his teeth together. And if he had taught her? Would he have scared her with his demands? His need for control? He'd been a baby Dom when she left, just twenty-one, and he knew only what his parents had taught him about a poly relationship. Since then, he'd learned what it meant to be a good Dominant. But the moment he saw her, his emotions took over.

"Just because she knew the one word to stop us cold doesn't mean she's fully educated." Jed leaned against a shelving unit, taking deep breaths, watching Ry. Ry

15

reached down and adjusted himself. It was then Ry noticed Jed's cock was as hard as his. "Information about safe words and hard limits is easy enough to find on the internet."

Ry blew out a breath. "Damn, you're right." He rubbed the back of his neck. "It's just the thought of another man…" His teeth snapped together, and Jed winced at the sound.

"Yeah, I'm with you there." Jed rubbed his stomach. "If another man has taught her, we will deal with it. She's been gone eight years. We can't expect her not to have experimented. It's not like we were celibate while she was gone."

"I lose all reason when I'm around her."

"You always did, and that's why you have me." Jed punched him in the arm, and they both smiled. "Shall we discuss how we want to handle Katie tomorrow?"

"Yes, when we get home. Because this time, I'm not letting her run."

Chapter 3

The next evening, Katie shut the front door of her grandmother's house with a sigh. She was late for her meeting with Ry and Jed.

She jogged to her car, hopped in, and took off. She'd hoped to walk to Ry and Jed's house, but it wasn't going to happen now. She didn't need more time to think. She'd thought of nothing but Ry and Jed and their reaction to her words since the pantry incident yesterday.

She reviewed some of the basics in her head while she drove, such as what she'd learned about BDSM and the poly lifestyle while she was in New York. Ry and Jed were both dominant males, and she would have to deal with that. But she wasn't going to be a pushover, either. There would be limits and rules. Katie had a submissive side, but it was mainly in the bedroom, not in life.

All too soon, she pulled into the driveway. Climbing out of her car, she shut the door and stood there for a minute as her pulse roared in her ears. No time like the present. She made her way to the front door, drew in a breath, and knocked.

The door opened to reveal Jed, wearing nothing but a pair of jeans. Her mouth went dry at the sight of his toned body. "Come on in, Kitty Kat."

Her heart hiccupped. Kitty Kat. Only Jed called her that.

"Thanks." She slipped through the opening as Jed pulled a black T-shirt over his head. Ry was standing across the room. He wore jeans as well, along with a tight tank top that did nothing to hide his muscular body. She swallowed. His six-pack abs were even more defined than Jed's. Her palms itched to touch him, to see if those muscles were as hard as they looked.

"You're late." Ry's voice was low and heavy.

"Yes." Her chin went up. She wasn't going to apologize.

"Bad move." Jed's spoke softly in her ear as his arms encircled her.

"I haven't given my consent to anything."

Jed held his hands up. "You're right."

Ry shook his head. "Let's talk." He gestured to the sofa.

"Come sit down." Ry patted the center of the sofa on the other side of the room.

When had he moved? Katie shook off the sensual cobwebs and sauntered over to the sofa. She sat, leaving space between her and Ry. Jed grinned at her as he strode over, nudged her to the middle, and took his seat. His thigh brushed hers.

Ry shifted, his hip bumping into hers as he scooted closer to her. Her body temperature shot up. Two men, two hard bodies.

Stay calm, you can handle this. She settled back and waited.

"One rule we have is we don't tolerate lateness. If you're late again, it will be five swats from the implement of our choice from each of us for every minute you're late." Ry placed his arm around her shoulders. "And we'll do it on your bare ass."

She nodded, twisting her fingers together, wishing her pussy didn't cream at his words. She should be frightened, but she wasn't. This was Ry and Jed. The two who had taken her the day after her eighteenth birthday, showing her sexual heights unmatched since.

"Are you nervous, Kitty Kat?" Jed asked.

"A little." She wasn't going to lie.

Ry opened his mouth, but the ringing of the landline caused him to swear. They had to keep a landline because cell coverage on the ranch could be spotty, and Jed wanted to be sure his crew could reach him.

"I'll get it." Jed rose, ambled over, and snatched up the receiver. "Yes." His lips pressed together. "Understood. I'll be right down." He hung the phone up and stared at her. "Misty's in trouble. I have to go down to the stables."

"Take care of her," Ry said.

Jed nodded. "Go ahead and continue. I'll catch up when I get back." He turned and walked to the back of the house.

"Tell me, Katie. How many men have you been with?" Ry asked.

"Four." Katie squirmed. She included him and Jed in that four. He didn't have to know her relationship with Walter was platonic. And the other was a Dom at the club who only played with her. No sex involved. She didn't want them to think she was totally inexperienced, even if she was.

"Are you saying—"

"Yes, that includes you and Jed." No hiding, she told herself. When she made her decision to leave New York, it was with the knowledge Ry and Jed were the only two men she wanted. Her father could go to hell and back for his ideas on who was a good man for his daughter. He'd pushed Walter at her every chance he got, and Walter wasn't the right man for her. Never had been.

"Then Jed was right. You know very little about our world."

"More than you think." Katie gathered up her courage. "Just because I didn't have intercourse doesn't mean I didn't play."

Ry sprung off the couch as if the fabric burned him. "You played? Where and with who?"

"Ry." She reached out and took his fist in her hand. He stiffened. Was she breaking an unspoken rule? But they hadn't established any rules yet, except if she was late. "This is something we can discuss when Jed is here. I don't want to explain twice."

And she didn't. She'd waited until she was twenty-two before she went to a club in New York. It had been more than to satisfy her curiosity, and to help her understand the lifestyle. Even if it scared the crap out of her at times.

But she was learning to deal with her fear. It was more fear of her own sexuality and learning to understand the needs she had. She trusted Ry and Jed. Her therapist Pamela had told her trust and communication was the foundation for any relationship. Something her father broke over and over again.

She waited, and Ry let out a breath. She pulled her arm back as he sat down.

"You know I've always been a little protective where you're concerned."

"A little." She laughed. "Remember when you punched Billy because he dared to steal a kiss in the ninth grade?"

Ry smiled. "Billy kissed all the girls. I wanted to be your first kiss."

Katie relaxed for the first time that night. "You were. Remember you kissed me at my fourteenth birthday party?"

"Yes, I did." He chuckled before capturing her hand and placing it on his thigh, trapping it under his. "Let's talk about limits."

She blinked at the change of subject.

"Looks like I'm back time for the good stuff," Jed said as he strode into the room. His dark T-shirt smeared with dirt.

"Misty okay?" Ry asked.

"Yep, doc has it handled." Jed dropped down onto the chair. "Misty is one of my mares. She's due to foal soon, and it hasn't been easy on her."

Katie smiled. "So you still love horses."

"Yes. There are some loves that never go away." Jed leaned forward, resting his elbows on his knees.

"Do you have any objections to rope bondage, the use of handcuffs or other restraints?" Ry asked.

"No, as long as it's not painful."

"Tell me what toys you've used." Ry's voice deepened.

She bit her lip, feeling a little embarrassed. "Dildo, vibrator, nipple rings, and a small butt plug."

"Used them on yourself or someone used them on you?"

"Both." Katie peeked at him from beneath her lashes.

He frowned. Katie opened her mouth, and he tapped her lips with his finger. "It's okay. As Jed pointed out, it has been eight years. While I don't like the idea of you with another man, I can understand it. We haven't exactly been celibate."

Katie squeezed his thigh. "Understood."

"I'm guessing spankings are okay since you didn't object when we said that's how we would punish you for being late."

"I don't mind being spanked, but what kind of implements are you talking about?"

"Maybe a better question is what kind of implements have you used?" Jed asked.

Her breath caught in her throat, and she had to force the words out. "Mainly different floggers. I don't want any welts or blood. That's a hard limit." She was amazed at how steady her voice was.

"Agreed," Ry said.

"As far as sex, what won't you do?" Jed asked.

"I'm not sure I understand what you mean." She tilted her head, looking at Jed. What kind of sex were they thinking of?

"Sex without a condom?" Ry asked.

"We can provide you with health reports to show we're negative for STIs," Jed said.

Katie took a deep breath, trying to calm the fire racing through her veins at the thought of their bare cocks in her pussy. "I'm on birth control, but I'd prefer a condom for any anal sex."

The men looked at each other, and Ry nodded. "We can live with that."

"Do you have any objection to fellatio?" Jed asked.

"No."

"What about same gender?" Ry asked.

Katie shook her head. "Hard limit. No same sex for me." Women just didn't do it for her; she had learned that in the New York club.

"Will you take both of us at the same time?" Jed asked. His gaze held hers. "One in the pussy and one in the ass?"

Her eyes closed then reopened, her heart racing liked she'd run a marathon. "Yes." Sandwiched between their two hard bodies… Oh yeah, her pussy pulsed at the idea.

"Do you fantasize?" Jed asked.

Her face went hot. "Yes."

"Will you let us act out those fantasies with you, Kitty Kat?" Jed asked.

"Yes," she whispered, but a grin played around her lips. Jed had given her the nickname Kitty Kat when he found her sunbathing nude when she was sixteen. He told her she'd stretched out like a cat sunning itself.

"So far we're very compatible," Ry said. "There are things Jed and I won't do." He paused, and Jed nodded. "No blood, no welts, no breath play, no medical play, no knives or cutting, no fire play, branding, electrical shock, or fisting. We do limited suspension, but we will work up to that."

"Sounds fair." Katie couldn't believe how calmly they were discussing this. Eight years ago, she would have run for the hills. Now…part of her still wanted to run, but the other part couldn't wait to get started. Her trust in Ry and Jed was unwavering; it was her fear of not being the woman they really wanted and needed that held her back.

"We'll keep to club safe words. *Red* will stop all play. *Yellow*, we will slow down and talk you through it. But only red will stop us. Are you okay with that?"

"I can agree to that."

"Any medical issues we need to know about?" Ry asked.

"No."

"Good." Ry leaned back. "There is something else we need to cover. Protocols."

"One of our required protocols is you will be on time," Jed said.

"I figured that one out." Katie squirmed.

"The next protocol involves the dungeon," Ry said.

"Dungeon? You have a dungeon?" How hard into play were these two? Okay, she'd heard the rumors as a teenager about how Ry's parents and Jed's father lived together, but never really believe it. When Ry and Jed came to her the day after her eighteenth birthday and told her what they wanted, after their one—and only—night together, she began believing the rumors.

Then the next morning, her father had shown up and encouraged her to leave for New York City with him. What a mistake that had been. Her father hadn't changed, not one bit.

"Yes, and that's where we will play," Jed said.

"Most of the time," Ry added. "When you come over, you will go down to the dungeon and remove your clothing."

"If you haven't already showered and shaved you can do so in the bathroom in there," Jed said. "There is a special mat for our submissive to stand on."

"We want you to stand straight and tall, hands resting at the small of your back, legs shoulder-width apart." Ry's voice was strong. "Eyes straight ahead. When we enter the room, you will keep the position until we tell you to move."

Katie licked her lips and closed her eyes. Her muscles quivered as she centered herself. Not high protocol, but nothing she couldn't deal with. "I can handle that." Even as she said the words, a shiver of anticipation flowed through her along with a sliver of doubt. What happened if she made a mistake? Or forgot to do something?

"Once we tell you to move, you may look at us," Jed said. "In the dungeon, you will call us Sir or Sir Ry and Sir Jed. We'll call you Katie, Kitty Kat, sweetheart or any other endearment we choose."

"Oh, and to add to the fun, if there is an outfit laid out on the bed, you will put it on before you get into position. No matter what the outfit is," Ry said.

Katie nodded, not trusting her voice.

"We will never hurt you," Jed said.

More doubts crowded her mind. She wasn't worried about them hurting her—they wouldn't. In her heart and brain she knew this. But what if she couldn't be the woman they needed? Would she end up hurting them? How much had she hurt them already by leaving? They needed to clear the air on that matter.

"But I hurt you both when I ran away," she blurted out.

Both men frowned. "I take responsibility for that," Ry said.

Her gaze darted between the two men, unsure of their mood.

"I think we both have to take responsibility," Jed said.

"You weren't ready for us, Katie. And we pushed," Ry said.

"We took your virginity," Jed said

"But I wanted you to." Her face grew warm after she said the words, but she wouldn't recall them. She had enjoyed her time with them.

"I think we overwhelmed you that night," Jed said, running a finger down her warm cheek.

Katie started to shake her head, but Ry cupped her

neck. "You left the next day, baby. No explanation, no anything."

"Okay, maybe I was a bit overwhelmed, but my leaving wasn't just because of what happened that night." And that was true. A heaviness settled in her chest.

"Will you tell us why you left?" Jed asked.

"Not tonight." She believed them when they said they presumed they overwhelmed her; it was the logical conclusion when she'd left the very next day. While she wanted to get this out, she wasn't sure she was ready to admit her gullibility. When Ry started to open his mouth, Katie shook her head. "Please? I will tell you, just not tonight." She rubbed her palm between her breasts, trying to ease the ache before dropping her hand to her lap.

Ry's breath caressed her cheek. "You are precious to us, Katie." He scooted closer. "We may push your limits a bit, but never with pain or something that is a hard limit." Ry pressed his chest against her right arm.

"We just want you to be ours, Kitty Kat." Jed turned, his fingers dancing over her shoulder and around her neck.

The heat from both men seared her skin, but she couldn't move. Fear and excitement flooded her entire being.

Her pussy clenched.

Her clit throbbed.

Her nipples hardened.

And her heart pounded.

"Shall we show you the dungeon, Katie?" Ry asked, his fingers playing with her hair.

Katie nodded.

"Oh, no, Kitty Kat," Jed said. "One more protocol—you will talk. Nodding will be accepted now and then, but you have to voice your wants, your needs, and your desires." Jed's touch disappeared.

"We want to hear your pleasure, your need, your excitement, and screams for us to do it harder and faster," Ry whispered. "Now stand up, my submissive." Ry scooted away from her on the sofa.

"Yes, Sir Ry." Katie pushed to her feet, amazed her legs held her up. She was a bundle of sexual nerves, and she had no idea of how long she could keep this up without going over the edge.

"First things first," Ry said, grabbing a straight back chair and carrying it over to her. He sat down and stared at her. "Bring her over here."

Oh, shit. Katie's breath caught in her throat.

Jed maneuvered her over to where Ry sat. "For being late, you will be spanked."

They were making good on their promise to punish her. A chill chased up her spine. She'd been spanked before.

She opened her mouth, but she couldn't think of anything to say. "Over my lap, baby." Ry patted his legs. Her heart pounded as she maneuvered herself onto Ry's lap.

Her pussy clenched. Ry's hand smoothed over her back, and Katie relaxed. Maybe they were just teasing her?

"Since this is our first time and we hadn't laid out the rules, you'll keep your jeans on and we each will do five swats." Ry's hand came down over her denim-covered ass.

"Ouch," she said, more out of surprise than pain. Four more times in rapid succession he swatted her ass. Her clothing took most of the impact, but it didn't stop the tingling from spreading from her ass to her clit. This was so very different from when she'd been spanked in the club. The club had been almost clinical, and she'd been accused more than once about being in her head too much. Ry's spanking made her shiver from anticipation, and there was no worry about the pain.

"My turn," Jed said.

"Stand up and then lie down over Jed's lap." Ry's voice was hoarse and stern.

Taking a shaky breath, Katie rose and waited for the men to switch positions. How many times had she fantasized about them doing this to her? Especially in the club when she'd watched subs get spanked, flogged, and caned. She'd only allowed one person at the club to spank her, and she'd never had this reaction.

Jed sat down, and she lay over his lap with an excited quiver tumbling in her stomach. Five more swats and he was done. Excitement flowed through her veins. What else would this night bring?

Ry grasped her by the shoulders and helped her stand. She wobbled on her feet for a few seconds when Ry let her go. Her panties were soaked, her clit pulsing with need. Damn, that hadn't happened the other times she'd been spanked. She never had an inkling it could be this exciting except in her fantasies.

"Okay?" Jed asked, running his finger down her cheek.

Heat flared over her face. "Yes," she whispered.

"Time to see our dungeon, Kitty Kat." Jed stood and walked across the living room. Katie followed him down the hall, hearing Ry's heavy footfalls on the hardwood floor behind her.

Shivers chased up and down her spine. When they reached a door, Jed punched the keypad on the wall until an electronic beep sounded.

"We'll give you the code," Ry said.

"Is it…" Katie cursed silently as she stumbled over what she wanted to say. "Is it always locked, Sir Jed?"

"Yes." Jed gave her a grin. "Be careful on the stairs." He opened the door and turned on the lights.

Katie gripped the railing for dear life. What was she doing? She fought an internal battle with her fears down each step until they came to the bottom of the staircase. The room was dark.

"Welcome to our dungeon and our world," Ry said before the room was filled with muted light.

Her jaw dropped open. The room was huge, and it was… Her mind went blank.

Chapter 4

Ry kept his gaze on Katie as her green eyes grew wide, and she blinked several times. She wasn't running away screaming…yet. He tried to rein in his thoughts. Katie was here. That's what mattered.

He was still a little unsettled over not having the conversation about why she left eight years ago. There were still some things they needed to work out. And that being the case, why were they here in the dungeon? Because Ry wanted to show her more of their world. She'd mentioned a club in New York, so some of this equipment should be familiar.

"Does it run the full length of the house?" She still stood in the doorway.

"Yes," Jed said, glancing over at Ry.

"From one end to the other. Our fathers built it," Ry said, trying to concentrate on the room rather than his raging cock. What would she think of the dual cross frame across the room, the bed off to the side, and the cabinets filled with their toys? Would everything scare her or make her tremble with excitement?

"And we've done some upgrades," Jed said.

"Like what?" Katie took a couple of steps into the room, and Ry let out a relieved breath.

So far, so good. He saw a confidence in Katie that hadn't been there when she was eighteen. He liked it.

"It's been soundproofed, has a state-of-the-art sound system, plus it holds all our toys and stuff," Ry said, running his fingers through his hair. Why was he so apprehensive? Maybe because he and Jed had never shared their dungeon with anyone but each other.

If they needed to play with a woman together, they went to the club several cities away and played there. In their home, it had only been the two of them. And it wasn't as if they hadn't dated women. They had. But now, the only woman he wanted in his life was Katie.

"Why don't you do the full tour, Ry," Jed said.

"Sure." Jed wanted him to lead, and as the primary Dominant, he should. Ry approached Katie and held out his hand. Soft skin met his as their fingers entangled. Joy sang through his veins. "You can ask any questions you want, and for tonight, there is no need to use the Sir title." He guided her over to the wall of shelves.

"Toys," she whispered. "You could open an adult store with what you have here."

"More than likely." Ry pulled her in front of him so her back rested against his chest. He needed her close. "We have gels and oils here along with dildos, vibrators, clamps, cock rings, cock toys, anal plugs and toys, and all sorts of insertables." He glanced over at Jed and mouthed, "Okay to tell her?"

Jed nodded.

"Everything to satisfy both the man and the woman in my life," Ry added.

"You mean…" Her eyes widened, before she looked at Jed, only to return her gaze back to him. "I never realized. I know you two are close, but…" Color flooded her cheeks.

"Jed and I play together, yes," Ry said. His assumption she'd heard the rumors about them when she was younger wasn't true. It wasn't a bad thing because he wasn't going to hide anything from her.

"He doesn't allow me to fuck him," Jed said.

"That's because you love it when I ream your ass." Ry almost laughed when Katie's eyes widened even more. Maybe it was because they'd each taken a turn with her that night but didn't touch each other. That had been difficult.

"So damn true," Jed said with laugher in his voice.

"I…" Katie closed her eyes and then opened them, meeting his gaze head on. "Okay, I can handle toys."

Ry brushed his lips against her temple. She hadn't said she accepted him and Jed being together. His throat constricted. "What about us?" What if she couldn't accept it? Would she understand that to accept one, she had to accept them both?

Katie blew out a breath. "I have to get used to the idea, but I'm not opposed."

"Thank fuck," Jed murmured.

Ry continued with the tour. "The whips, floggers, canes, shackles, cuffs, and spreader bars are all hung up on the wall. There are rings in all the walls, the ceiling, and the floor, so we can tie you up any way we want you."

Katie's breathing turned rapid, and Ry smiled. "The bathroom is in the corner." He maneuvered her body so she could see it.

"There's no door."

"No, it's totally open so we can see you at all times, and you can see us." Loosening his hold around her waist, he guided her to where Jed stood.

"And this is our play furniture," Jed said, taking a position to Katie's right.

"Our bed is specially made to accommodate three people." Ry placed his hand on one of the frame posts. He wondered if this was all too much for her. "The frame is metal. Think of how it will feel to be on that bed, tied up, and being fucked by us."

Ry heard a puff of breath leave Katie's lips and saw how flushed her skin was. Yes, she was getting excited. Good. That's what he wanted.

"Here," Jed said. Keeping Katie between them, they maneuvered her to the chair. "You'll be bound, where you will be teased, played with, and fucked."

Katie swayed on her feet, but they kept her upright between them. Her breathing was choppy as he gazed at her face. No distress showed in her eyes. Only fire burned in their depths.

"We'll lay you across this spanking horse and give you such a good whipping, you'll orgasm."

"Or it can be used to fuck you as well, both in the pussy and ass," Ry said before he led her to her right for the next piece of equipment. "The wood frame is one of our newer additions. We can tie you in the middle of it and have lots of fun."

"And depending on how we're feeling that night," Jed said, picking up where Ry left off, "we can torment you for hours."

This time, Katie shifted from one foot to the other, then back again. Her breathing increased, and her fingers stroked the seam of her jeans on her thigh.

"And next is my favorite," Jed said. "The prison stockade."

"Crap," she whispered, her gaze on the polished metal resting on the floor. "I wasn't expecting something so…medieval."

Ry chuckled. "We'll work up to this. I can put you or Jed on your hands and knees, lock you into position, and maybe restrain your head."

"Or we can hook up a dildo to the fucking machine," Jed commented.

"And we can set it fast or slow." Ry paused for a moment. "Or maybe one day, I'll let you watch while I have the fucking machine take Jed's ass."

Katie gasped, and her gaze went to Jed, who was grinning.

Were they shocking her? Probably. But he wasn't going to hide his relationship with Jed. Or who he was.

"Bring it on," Jed said.

"You're tempting me, Jed." Ry's laughter filled the air as he threw his arm around Katie's shoulders.

"And you love to be tempted."

A fine shiver shook Katie. Maybe they needed to discuss his and Jed's relationship a bit more. But he couldn't believe that Katie hadn't seen a male sub and male Dom before. He opened his mouth to check in with her.

Jed shook his head, but Ry ignored him. "You still okay about us?"

"I'm fine." Her voice was soft, but there was no fear or distress in her eyes.

"Then let's keep going," Jed commented keeping his gaze on Katie.

"Our next fun item is the fucking stool," Ry said. It was the standard bar stool height. The hole in the middle of the seat allowed the dildo to be attached, and the motor under the legs controlled the dildo.

"You've got to be kidding," Katie said.

"No, sweetheart," Ry said. "This stool was specially made. Depending on the dildo we choose to put on it, we can make it a punishment or pleasure."

"Or you can watch me as I take it up my ass, as I come all over your breasts or in your mouth," Jed said.

Ry glanced sharply at Jed before his gaze went to Katie. Her lips were parted, her skin flushed. She didn't seem upset, maybe a bit turned on. It seemed Jed wasn't going to censor his words anymore. Good.

"And while he's being fucked by it, I can take your ass," Ry whispered. His cock pulsed with need. But it would have to wait.

Another shiver went through her, but this time, when her gaze met Ry's, her pupils were dilated with lust. He turned her to face another table. "This is the massage table."

Katie let out a shaky laugh, and Ry chuckled.

"Don't let it fool you," Ry said. "We can use it to massage you with oil or to loosen tense muscles after you've been tied up."

"And we can use it to tease you." Jed ran his fingers over her arm.

"Or simply pull you to the edge and fuck you."

She sucked in a breath, and Ry grinned, taking her hand. "Do you want to stop?"

"No. Finish up. I want to know what I'm getting into."

"Plus, we have swings and all sorts of ways to tie you up, tease you until you're begging us to fuck you, or withhold your orgasm from you." Jed said.

Ry looked at Jed, and he nodded. Together they released her and stepped away.

"This is what it means to belong to us, Katie," Ry said, watching her face closely. He didn't see any distress or panic.

"And now is the decision time. Are you willing to accept all of this and us?" Jed asked.

Ry fought against snatching her up against his chest and holding her to him. She had to make the decision; he wouldn't force her.

"If you stay, it's accepting both of us into your life, your body, and your mind," Ry said. "We will be your Sirs here in the dungeon, in our home, and on our property."

"And if you choose to go, then that's the end of it. We won't ever mention this again," Jed said.

Ry didn't even want to contemplate Katie leaving. "We need a decision, Katie," Ry said. His heart pounded as he waited for her to answer.

Her gaze switched from him to Jed and back again. Her body trembled. He held his breath while Jed went still.

"We keep this between us, right? No other parties involved?"

"Yes," Jed said.

"You said 'the property'. Define what you mean. I won't parade around naked for others."

"Fuck, no, you won't," Ry said. "Only we get the pleasure of seeing you naked."

"What we meant is if we go on a picnic on the property, or we're in the stables, if we tell you to strip, then you will. We will always protect you from prying eyes."

"Are you expecting me to be your slave while I'm in your home?"

"Hell, no," Jed said.

"Never, Katie." Ry ran his finger over her cheek to reassure her. "We don't want a slave. We want a submissive who will obey us in all things sexual within her limits."

"I…" Her tongue darted out to moisten her lips, and she swallowed before glancing around the room. Her gaze returned to them. "I need to think."

There was total silence for a second or two before Jed cupped her chin.

"I understand." Jed kissed her forehead.

"Of course you do." Ry kissed her cheek.

"Let's go back upstairs and answer any questions you have before you go home." Jed took her arm and guided her upstairs, leaving Ry to follow.

* * * *

Katie tried to quell her riotous nerves when Jed led her to the sofa and sat down next to her. This is what she wanted. Two men to dominate her, to take control, to make her theirs. Ry came in a minute later and sat in a chair off to the side instead of sitting next to her.

Oh, hell. Was he upset with her? Was she messing up already? She'd heard the rumors about them and only half believed them. Their night together, they hadn't shown any sexual contact between them. Maybe because they were worried they'd frighten her off if they did.

Hell, she'd been a bit frightened about having a relationship with two powerful Dominants, but now… She wanted them. Knowing they were lovers didn't change her mind. It made her burn even hotter for the two of them.

As a kid, she'd heard about their parents, how they all lived together and loved each other. Jed's mom had died when Jed was six. His father had been grief-stricken, so Ry's mom had stepped in helping taking care of Jed. It surprised no one in town as the two couples had been long time friends and neighbors. When Jed turned fifteen, his dad and Ry's dad merged their two properties and built one big house.

She hadn't fully understood what it all meant until she was grown. Their parents had been living a poly lifestyle and had made it work.

Katie's gaze roamed over Ry's body, his cock hard under his jeans. But his fingers were curled into his palms. Well, this wasn't good.

"Did I do something wrong?" she asked, keeping her gaze locked on Ry.

Surprise registered in those dark eyes of his, then his lips turned up. "No, sweetheart." He shifted his legs before reaching down to adjust himself.

She squirmed in her seat. Her fingers itched to replace his. Her pussy clenched at the thought of touching these two men. And their dungeon? The toys, floggers, and whips created a firestorm within her. But it was the thoughts of the bed and the other equipment that threatened to consume her. She never expected to have this reaction. The club she went to in New York had had some basic items, but she'd never been so turned on by the idea of the items being used on her.

"I'm hard for you, Katie, and so is Jed."

Unable to help herself, she glanced at Jed's groin, and yep, his cock pressed against his pants too. Without thinking about it, Katie ran the tip of her finger over Jed's bulge.

"Fuck." Jed shifted his hips. "I'm so on the edge right now."

"And we still have things to discuss," Ry said. "Tell us about you playing in the club."

She'd wondered when he'd return to that topic. Sitting back against the sofa, Katie tried to relax. "At my dad's company, I met some of the other female workers. We usually went out for drinks on Friday night, just to unwind from the week. And one Friday night, we got to talking about sex." She tangled her fingers together in her lap.

"We discussed the usual stuff. Right after I turned

twenty-two, Jan approached me at lunch the following week and asked me if I was interested in the kinkier aspects of sex. When I told her maybe, she gave me a card. It had the name of Dr. Pamela Shaffer, Sexual Psychologist, and the date and address of her next free workshop."

"And you went?" Jed slipped his arm around her shoulders.

"Yes, I was curious. Pam was fantastic, and she opened my eyes to a lot of things. She gave me a list of recommended books to read, so I ordered them and read them."

"They helped?" Ry asked.

Katie's gaze caught his. Desire shined in his eyes. "Yes, I began to understand more about the lifestyle you two wanted. She took me under her wing after I explained about you two and my bad reaction."

"Aw hell, Kitty Kat, your reaction was natural. You were only eighteen."

"A very naïve eighteen."

"This Dr. Pam took you to clubs to play?" Ry asked.

"Sort of. She knew I wasn't ready to play but wanted to know more. She took me to clubs she knew were safe and would welcome me."

"And what did you think of the clubs?" Jed asked.

"At first, I was scared to death, but after the first couple of times—when no one minded that I stayed clothed or didn't participate—I began to watch and learn. And later, I participated on a limited basis."

"Tell me what you learned," Ry said.

Katie took a deep breath. "I learned I'm a sexual submissive, about the power exchange, and though my desires were different, they weren't any less important."

"You said you participated on a limited basis," Ry

said. "Explain."

"It means I allowed Sir William to play with my breasts, put clamps on them, and to spank me." Her gaze flickered to Jed, then back to Ry. Neither seemed upset by this. That made her relax a little more.

"And sex?" Jed asked.

Katie shook her head. Time to tell the truth. "No sex. Not since you two."

Ry sprang from his chair, and Katie winced. Oh, hell, she'd misread him. She'd told him earlier that she'd been with four men but hadn't mentioned sex. How angry was he she'd left that detail out? It was hard to tell.

"Ryland," Jed snapped.

Ry glanced at them, closed his eyes, then opened them. "Sorry, Katie, I'm not angry. I just can't believe you haven't had sex in eight years."

"I have used toys. I had to get some relief somehow."

"Of course you did." Jed squeezed her shoulders. "I think maybe this is enough for tonight."

Ry straightened and ran his fingers through his hair. "Dinner tomorrow night. Be here at six. We'll have dinner first. You can tell us how you're feeling and if you're ready to play with us. If the answer is yes, you'll go down to the dungeon, and we'll begin your training."

"Okay." Katie stood up, feeling confused but also relieved. She turned to Jed. "Tomorrow." She gave him a kiss on the cheek, then turned to Ry.

She didn't want Ry angry with her. It was up to her to show him the woman she'd become. She raised her chin and marched over to Ry. He went still when she stopped in front of him. "All I can say is I'm sorry I ran. I was too young to understand myself, let alone what the two of you needed." Standing on her toes, she kissed his cheek.

"I'll walk you out," Jed said as he took her hand.

She threw a glance over her shoulder, but Ry hadn't moved. She fought against saying something more. She didn't want this to be an upward battle.

Jed squeezed her hand as they walked out the front door. "All will be okay."

* * * *

Ry's fingers curled into his palms so he wouldn't grab Katie as he watched her leave. He didn't trust himself right now. Eight fucking years. He wasn't mad at her at all. He was mad at himself.

He'd never hurt her, not for all the money in the world. But he had. He only wanted to protect her, to take care of her, to make her his. He stayed where he was as Jed walked her out to her car. Ry heard her car start, and the engine noise faded as she drove away. The second Jed closed the door behind him, Ry stripped off his jeans and let out a breath of relief, giving his hard erection some room.

"No kidding," Jed said as he unzipped his pants and allowed his cock to hang out of his open jeans.

"Do you realize how hard it was for me to let her go tonight?"

"Yes." Jed stripped his clothes off and flopped down on the sofa.

"Earlier, when you were out, she told me she'd been with four men, including us. She let me think she'd had sex with other men."

Jed chuckled. "Can you blame her?"

"No, but if one man was Sir William, then who is the other guy?" Ry clenched his jaw.

"Probably someone her father picked out." Jed gave him a cheeky grin, his hand fisting his cock. "So, what's it going to be tonight?"

Some of the tension drained from Ry's muscles. Leave it to Jed. "Your ass is mine, so get your butt down to the dungeon and assume the position."

"Yes, Sir Ry. I'm more than ready for a hard cock up my ass." Jed stood and gave him a saucy salute.

"If you don't behave yourself, you'll get more than my cock."

"Tease."

Ry laughed, then followed Jed down to the dungeon. Tomorrow was going to be an interesting day.

Chapter 5

"What's for dinner?" Ry asked the next evening.

Jed straightened from the oven and turned to see Ry near the kitchen door. "Steak, potatoes, and broccoli." Ry's arms were crossed over his chest, his jaw clenched. Damn, this wasn't good. Was Ry worked up over tonight? "You need to chill, so go take a shower and change."

"It will be a quick one." Ry glanced at Jed with a slow smile taking over his lips.

Jed swore. He knew that look in Ry's eyes. If Katie wasn't coming over, and they had time… Jed grinned and then shook his head. "I know what you're thinking," he said, then laughed. "Go. Katie will be here shortly, and I know how you are on punctuality."

"Keep that up, Jed, and I'll fuck your ass even harder tonight."

"Ah, promises and more promises." Jed shook his finger at Ry.

Ry laughed as he left the kitchen.

Jed had finished setting the table when he heard Ry jogging down the stairs. Jed had made sure someone was on duty with the horses so they could play uninterrupted tonight. Not that he expected anything to go wrong with the horses.

The doorbell rang. Ry shot him a grin as he loped over to the door and pulled it open.

"Evening, Katie." Ry swept her into his arms and

kissed her.

A burning sensation started in Jed's stomach. He clenched his teeth. He'd taken two steps before he realized he'd moved. Hell. He forced himself to stop and take a breath, slowly unclenching his muscles. He hated that he was jealous. He'd have to talk to Ry about it. Katie was theirs, and he knew Ry would share.

"My turn." He pulled Katie out of Ry's arms and into his. Her mouth was warm and wet as their tongues dueled then tangled together.

God, her soft flesh molded to his hardness. He needed her so much. His cock twitched as she broke the kiss.

"No offense, but a girl needs to breathe now and then."

The timer on the stove went off, and Jed grinned. "Dinner. Ry, I'll let you seat Katie while I bring the food out."

"Of course," Ry said.

Jed strode into the kitchen and gripped the kitchen counter. He closed his eyes and swore softly as he fought against the jealousy crashing through his blood stream. It wasn't like they hadn't shared Katie before, and he'd kissed her right after Ry. He'd never reacted this way, so hard and so fast. But this was Katie. Forcing away the little green monster, Jed dished up dinner and carried the two platters and a bowl out to the table.

"Smells delicious," Katie said. Ry had seated her to his right.

"Jed is a wonder in the kitchen," Ry commented as Jed placed one platter heaped with potatoes on the table along with the bowl of broccoli.

Jed carried the other platter over to Katie then he set a piece of steak on her plate. The back of his hand brushed her breast. "Medium well, just like the lady likes."

He straightened then served Ry.

Decision time. Jed stood with platter in hand. Sit on Katie's right or on Ry's left where he normally sat? Hell, the table was set that way, but he could always move his plate.

"Jed." His head jerked up at Ry's firm voice. Ry stared at him, then tilted his chin up toward the chair on Ry's left.

Tension seeped out of his body as the decision was made for him. Ry was still his Dominant. Placing the last steak on his plate, Jed took his seat.

Katie cut into her steak. "You remembered."

"Of course I remembered. Who could ever forget your face when we went to dinner in Monroe, and you sent your steak back three times before they got it right."

"Well, I don't like my beef mooing."

Ry laughed. "I thought the waiter was going to kick us out."

"Yeah, and our fathers left a big tip."

The men sobered up for a minute and then smiled at Katie. "Our folks loved having you around," Ry said.

Katie reached out and touched Ry's hand where it rested on the table, and a surge of jealousy hit Jed again. Then Katie held her other hand out to him across the table, and he took it.

"Your family was always so welcoming and happy. I'm sorry they're gone." She squeezed his hand, and Jed's lips quirked.

"Me too," he whispered.

"It was an accident." Ry mumbled. "But they'd be happy to know you've come home."

Katie smiled then dished up her potatoes and

vegetables. "So, Ry, you're the sheriff now?"

Jed puffed out a breath, happy for the change in subject. He didn't want to dwell on the death of his father and Ry's parents.

"Yep, and if you step a toe out of line, into jail with you."

Katie laughed. "I'll be good. But"—she ducked her head almost shyly—"I got stopped on the way into town. Know anything about that?"

Ry grinned, and Jed barely kept a smile from his lips. "What did he stop you for? Speeding?"

"Littering," Katie muttered.

"Littering?" Jed barely suppressed his laughter.

"It's a serious offense." Ry grinned before he dug into his food. The subject was dropped.

"This is delicious," Katie praised after a few minutes of eating.

"I aim to please." Jed's ego swelled.

"Well, you always please me," Ry commented.

Katie's gaze clashed with Jed's, and Jed fought not to squirm in his seat. He had nothing to be embarrassed about. He and Ry had played together since they were eighteen. They'd experimented before that, but their parents asked them to wait until they were legal age.

"Umm… So, tell me about the horses." Katie voice was soft.

"One of my favorite topics." Jed was pleased that Katie wanted to know more about him. "I've got several horses in the stable. Mainly for breeding." He paused, wondering how much to tell her. In the years she'd been gone, between him and Ry, they'd acquired more land and made the ranch profitable.

"I remember you liked to teach people about horses

and riding."

He smiled. "Still do. I have smaller, gentler horses for the kids." Jed continued talking about his work with the kids while they ate. "Sounds like you're enjoying yourself," Katie remarked when he finished talking.

"It's a job I love." Jed lifted his chin. Katie was truly interested in him and what he was doing. His chest swelled.

Ry cleared his throat. "While we load the dishwasher, go down to the dungeon, Katie."

Jed recognized Ry going into Sir mode. His cock hardened.

Katie stood. "Yes, Sir."

And apparently, so did Katie. Good, she was getting it. "Door code is seventeen, thirty-six, twenty," Jed said.

Katie turned and left the room. Jed groaned before glancing at Ry. "Are you as hard as I am?"

"Yep." Ry ran his palm down his cock where it pressed against his sweats.

"I need to let you know something."

Ry's gaze jerked to Jed's face. "I'm not going to like this."

"When you kissed Katie earlier, the little green-eyed jealousy monster raised its head."

"Then I think we're even. It happened to me when you brushed your fingers over Katie's breast when you served her."

"How are we going to handle this?" He breathed a sigh of relief. He wasn't alone in this, and it made him feel better. "I've never been like this before."

"We'll take it one step at a time, be honest with ourselves and each other. Communication is going to be the key."

"Yes. I've always been submissive to you on a sexual level. But when we've been with a woman together, I've never had an issue with jealousy."

"Maybe because we never had feelings for anyone but Katie. She is ours. Ours together." Ry strode over and clasped Jed's shoulder. "No matter if we're with her together or we're alone with her. We both care about her."

"You make it sound so simple." Jed washed the dishes that couldn't go into the dishwasher as Ry finished loading the dishwasher and turned it on.

"It's a matter of reminding ourselves that we're in this together and talk to each other. I'm not saying we're not going to have issues, but we're all in this together."

Jed nodded. "Let's go see how our Kitty Kat has performed."

Chapter 6

Katie stood near the bed, staring at the stairs, forcing herself not to squirm. How long had it been? Five minutes? Ten minutes? She'd stripped off her clothes and put them on the side table as instructed. There was no outfit, so she stood totally naked, hands behind her back, legs spread, and eyes straight ahead.

Her insides quaked. Ry and Jed had told her what to expect, and they'd discussed it, but their dungeon still caught her by surprise. It was the most amazing dungeon she'd ever seen, and she'd visited several private ones when she was in New York.

Footsteps sounded on the stairs. Oh, God, they were coming. Her heart sped up, and she swallowed. The room temperature shot up when they entered. They moved out of her sight, and the padded floor of the dungeon muffled their footfalls.

Hands touched her shoulders, and she jumped.

"Shoulders back," Ry said, his palms on her shoulders, pulling them back.

"And feet farther apart." Jed put his foot in between hers and pushed until she widened her stance.

"Better," Ry said.

"Did you shower before you came over?" Jed asked.

Oh damn, she'd forgotten that part of their instructions. "No, Sir Jed."

"Go place yourself over the spanking horse," Jed said.

Katie bit her lower lip and walked over to the horse.

She'd heard the disappointment in Jed's tone, and it cut her to the bone. Could she do this? She had to try. Excitement and trepidation warred within her. Taking a deep breath, she knelt on the padded leg rest and lay on her stomach on the padded top bar. Her arms hung down along with her head. Her heart pounded; her pussy clenched, and her nipples hardened.

Confusion ran riot in her brain. How could she be so excited by this? She'd never felt like this level of excitement in the club she attended. Her pussy was wet and needy, wanting…she didn't know what. This was so different than how she'd reacted in the city. There it had all seemed so clinical, so boring. But not now. Her heart was going a mile a minute, and her nerves tingled with anticipation.

"Let's see… What shall we use?" Jed mused.

Katie tried to think back to what was hanging on the wall, but there had been so many things.

"This one," Ry said.

She wished she could see what the men had picked. If she turned around, she'd break another rule, and she didn't want to do that. One punishment would be enough for her.

"Spread those knees out. We want to see you as we spank you," Jed said.

"Yes, Sir Jed." Katie wiggled her knees outward on the extra wide leg rest, feeling the cool air caress her pussy lips. She fought with herself as part of her wanted to jump up and run while the other wanted to stay and make them proud of her.

"You will receive three spanks from each of us. Do not move your hands or your legs. Do not straighten or do anything that will prevent us from punishing you. Each infraction will double the punishment," Ry said.

"Yes, Sir Ry."

"Do you remember your safe words?" Jed asked.

"Yes, Sir Jed. Red and yellow." Katie took a deep breath to steel herself for the first blow, but nothing happened. She let out a breath and—

"Ahhh."

The smack itself wasn't hard at all, not any more than the spanking she'd received the other night. She clenched her fingers into her palms so she wouldn't reach back and cover her ass.

Two more smacks, then a slight pause. Katie fought to keep her position. Though she wanted to stand up, she knew they weren't done. Her ass was warm and tingling. Her clit throbbed, and her pussy clenched hard.

"Now my turn," Ry said.

Oh crap, she thought Ry had spanked her first. Ry struck her with more force. Not enough to cause her pain— just a stinging sensation—but damn if her pussy didn't clench tighter with each hit. By the third hit, her ass was hot, moisture coated her pussy, and she was panting.

"Good girl." Jed's hand caressed her ass.

"Very good." Ry's hand joined Jed's. Then his fingers slipped down and ran over her slit.

"You liked that," Jed said.

"Yes, Sir Jed, I did." She wasn't going to lie. When she had experienced it with Sir William, it had been more clinical. And she'd wondered why people enjoyed it. Now, she understood. She needed to be with someone who excited her, someone who cared about her, and someone she trusted.

"Straighten up and look at your ass," Ry ordered.

Katie leaned back and looked over her. Ry held a mirror even though there was a full-sized mirror across the room so she could see her pink ass. She wanted to touch it to see if it felt as hot as it looked.

"We used the fur-covered paddle this time." Jed held it up so she could see it. "But next time, we'll use a different paddle."

Oh, God, how would a regular paddle feel?

"Go get on the bed and lay on your back, arms over your head and legs spread." Ry waved his hand toward the bed.

Katie kept her gaze on the two men as she walked to the bed. Jed put the paddle back, and Ry went to one of the drawers. If she remembered right, that drawer held all the insertable toys. Climbing on the bed, she did as Ry asked.

A small shiver of excitement slid over her skin. What were they planning next? Apprehension entered her veins. Could she really do this? Her hot and tender ass against the cool sheets reminded her of what would happen if she disobeyed.

They both appeared in her vision.

"Tomorrow night, you will be here at five-thirty. We will have dinner, and after dinner, we play," Jed said.

"I promised to have dinner with gran tomorrow." Her voice as soft.

"Then be here by seven and go to the dungeon," Jed replied.

"In the meantime…" Ry's hands were at her pussy, opening her lips, and pushing something into her soaked channel. "I've put four weighted balls into your pussy. You are to keep them in except if they cause you pain and to clean them a couple times a day to prevent an infection. We will remove them tomorrow night."

"Sir Ry?" The metal balls were cold, but her wet pussy warmed them up.

"Yes."

"What happens if they fall out?"

"You will keep count of how many times they fall out, and you will wash them and put them back in."

"Keep clenching those pussy muscles, that will keep them in," Jed said.

"And do not pleasure yourself. You are not to come. If you do come, keep track, because you will be punished for each time you come without permission."

"Yes, Sirs." Oh, God, how the hell was she going to survive? Her pussy was already clenching the toy, and her clit throbbed with need. They were asking for the impossible.

"Now close your legs and lower your arms."

The second she lowered her arms, the men were on either side, cuddling with her. Aftercare. She remembered this from the club. After a scene, she'd watch the Doms cuddle with their subs, giving them water and making sure they were okay.

"You are so very wet, Katie. You enjoyed what we did tonight." Ry's lips caressed her shoulder.

"Yes, Sir Ry, I did enjoy it, although…" Jed's fingers began toying with her nipple.

"Although what?" Jed asked.

"I was very nervous at first. I haven't been naked in front of either of you in a long time."

"You did very well," Ry said, his lips near her ear. "Trust your instincts, Katie, and talk to us."

The men kissed and petted her for a while before Jed declared they needed to call it an evening. She was nice and relaxed, just lying there in their arms. She enjoyed their brand of aftercare.

Katie climbed off the mattress and moaned. The

movement of getting to her feet caused the balls to shift in her pussy, and they expected her not to climax for twenty-four hours? Already her pussy was straining against the balls.

She reached for her clothing. She picked up her panties then paused.

"Need help?" Jed plucked her panties from her fingers and knelt in front of her. "Lift your foot." He tapped her right ankle.

Katie started to lift her foot but needed something to hold on to.

"Allow me." Ry's hands framed her waist. "I've got you."

Her right foot lifted maybe an inch, and Jed slipped her panties over her foot, then waited until she changed feet and did the same maneuver. His fingers brushed against her calves as he pulled her panties up. She bit back a moan of pleasure.

"Hand me her bra," Ry said.

Jed snagged the lacy fabric and placed it into Ry's outstretched hand. Ry's chest pressed against her back as he held the bra in his hands. "Put your arms in the straps."

She followed his directions, all while trying to control her breathing. She'd never had a man dress her before. Ry expertly slid the straps up, fastened the bra, and lifted her breasts into the cups.

"Perfect," he whispered against her ear as his fingers trailed over her hard nipples.

Unable to help herself, she shifted from one foot to the other and let out a gasp as the balls shifted within her core.

"I think for the jeans you need to be sitting down." Jed gestured toward the bed, and Katie sat on the mattress.

The two men finished dressing her quickly without

jostling her too much. "Are you going to be okay to drive?" Jed asked.

With a groan Katie stared at Jed. "I walked here." There was no way she could walk all the way back to Gran's house with those balls torturing her with each step.

"We'll drive you home," Ry said.

"Okay." She took a step then stopped. Damn, how was she going to get anything done? "Umm… Sirs?" She went back to formality.

"What is it, Kitty Kat?"

"I don't know if I'll be able to walk, let alone function, with the balls teasing me."

Jed glanced up at Ry.

"This is part of your training, little one." Ry's hands settled on her shoulders and rubbed them gently. "You have control over your body, but since this is your first time with them, if they get too overwhelming, call one of us."

"Yes, Sir." She closed her eyes, took a deep breath, let it out, and straightened her spine. "I'm ready."

"That's my girl." Ry's breath brushed against her ear. "But I'm not going to make it that hard on you."

Katie let out a small squeal when Ry scooped her up into his arms and carried her out of the dungeon.

Jed started laughing as he followed them up the stairs and grabbed the keys to his truck. "I guess I'd better drive since you have your hands full."

Five minutes later, she was standing at her front door, waving Ry and Jed off. Now to just make it inside the house and upstairs to her room.

* * * *

Ry and Jed sat in the truck, watching Katie stroll up the walkway to her home. Her steps were slow and measured, and Jed would bet his best breeding mare that Katie's pussy was sopping wet and clenching those balls to keep them in. To make sure she didn't disappoint them by allowing them to fall out.

"Finally," Ry said as Katie pushed open the front door and stepped into the house. He didn't know how much more he could take, watching her struggle.

"I think our phones are going to be ringing shortly." Jed's fingers curled around the steering wheel. "Do you think she will accept us?" Jed drove his truck away from the curb.

Silence answered him. Then Ry rubbed the back of his neck. "I believe she will, but she's a little overwhelmed."

"But if she doesn't?" Jed wasn't willing to give Katie up, but could he give up Ry's brand of loving? Ry offered him the domination he craved, but he was a switch and got off on dominating Katie. Could he go back to a non-touching relationship with Ry? They'd have to touch when they made love to Katie together. His thoughts twirled in circles.

"Let's cross that bridge when we get to it."

"But—"

Ry's phone rang, cutting him off. "What's up, Katie?" Ry asked, putting the phone on speaker.

Jed made a mental note to talk to Ry about this again. Ignoring it wasn't going to fix the issue, if there was one.

"Um, Sir, I really need to remove the balls to get to my bedroom."

"Where are you?"

"Downstairs bathroom." The tension in her voice spoke volumes. "I really want to please you both, but my body is on edge."

"Okay, sweetheart. Put your phone on speaker and set

it on the sink."

"Yes, Sir."

Jed glanced at him. "What do you have in mind?" he whispered.

Ry put his finger over the mouthpiece of his cell. "I'm going to have Katie take the balls out while we listen."

Jed twisted in his seat. They could hear fumbling noises on the other end.

"Okay, Sir. Phone on sink."

"Good girl. Can you get undressed?"

"I think so, Sir." The rustling of clothing could be heard. "Pants and underwear off."

Jed shifted in his seat again. His cock strained against his jeans.

"Now reach between your legs and spread your pussy lips." There was silence then a small gasp. "Move your fingers around until you find a small string."

"Have it, Sir." Her voice was a little breathless.

"Pull the balls out, one by one, Katie. Counting them as you do so."

"One." A louder gasp, this time. "Two." Then she let out a groan. "Three." A moan this time.

Jed's dick pulsed. If he released his cock and gave it stroke, he'd come right there in the truck.

There was a pause, and Ry opened his mouth. But before he could say anything, Katie's voice came through loud and clear. "Oh, fuck. Yes." Loud panting. "Four is out."

"Did you just come, Katie?"

"Yes, Sir, I did." There was no regret in her voice, only pleasure.

Jed bit back his laughter.

"Go to bed, but you're to put the balls back in before

you go to sleep."

"Yes, Sir. Thank you, Sir." The line went dead.

Ry let his head fall back against the truck seat. "I need some relief."

Jed glanced down. Ry's erection clearly outlined by the fabric of his jeans. "Let's get into the house." They both bailed out of the truck. Jed ambled toward the house, and Ry fell in step right beside him, their gaits slower than normal. They were both fighting massive erections. Once inside the house, Jed pushed Ry up against the front door and dropped to his knees.

"Mine," he whispered, lowering the zipper on Ry's jeans and releasing his hard dick.

Jed's hot mouth enveloped his cock, and Ry groaned. Jed sucked deep. He loved Ry's spicy flavor. Hell, who was he kidding? He loved Ry, period. He loved serving his Sir, how he could make Ry groan and shout.

Ry's fingers tangled in Jed's hair as he started to fuck his mouth. Jed relaxed his throat, taking all of Ry's cock. Ry let out a moan, and contentment filled Jed. He wanted nothing more than to please Ry.

Jed lifted his right hand off Ry's thigh and began playing with Ry's balls. Ry shifted his hips in reaction, and if Jed could have smiled, he would have.

How would Katie's mouth feel wrapped around his throbbing dick? Would she accept him and Ry playing together, fucking together? God, he hoped so, because he didn't think he could give Ry up.

Jed's cock throbbed as he continued to pleasure Ry, to give his Sir satisfaction. All too soon, Ry let out a shout and shot down his throat.

Jed twirled his tongue around Ry's cock, enjoying his salty taste, knowing he'd done a good job. They were both pretty worked up after playing with Katie. Jed wondered how they would survive until they could fuck her. In the meantime… He licked the head of Ry's cock and let it slip from his mouth. He grinned at Ry.

Ry's dick was already hardening again. It was going to be a long night. One he looked forward to.

Jed unzipped his jeans to give his own erection some breathing room before he stripped out of his clothing. "I'll be waiting in the dungeon." He stood and jogged down to the room, his cock bobbing. Once in the dungeon, he glanced at all the equipment until he found what he wanted. He sauntered over to the kneeling stocks.

Taking the top off the stocks, he set the wooden top down. He knelt on the padded seat, leaning forward until his chest rested on the upper piece. He put his head and arms in the stock and waited.

Ry's swift intake of breath had Jed's cock jumping. A soft hand caressed his ass before the stocks were locked into place. He was captured. Pressure on the inside of his thighs had him widening his legs as much as he could on the seat.

"Now that I have you at my mercy, what shall I do with you?" Ry asked.

"Whatever you want, Sir." Jed wiggled his butt.

Ry slapped his ass with an open hand, causing Jed to gasp, his ass stinging. "That's right, my little obedient sub."

Jed couldn't see what Ry was doing, but he heard the opening and closing of the drawers. He took a calming breath. He needed relief, and Ry would give it to him. Ry would make him feel so good and ease the ache inside him.

"First things first." The noise of the shelf unhooking caused Jed to glance at Ry and then back down. Ry lowered the shelf right below Jed's groin. Jed clenched his hands. What did Ry have in store for him?

Ry's fingers curled around Jed's cock, stroking and pulling as if he wasn't hard enough already. Then Ry slipped a penis sleeve onto Jed's dick and set it on the specially built shelf that was part of the equipment, which was at the perfect level to torment Jed with the toy.

Oh, fuck. Ry wasn't going to go easy on him. Not that he wanted him to, but he hadn't expected this.

The sound of a cap being popped reached his ears.

Cool liquid hit his ass, then Ry's fingers were there. Relaxing his muscles, Jed closed his eyes as Ry pushed one lubed finger up deep inside him. Ry added another finger, stretching his opening and spreading the lube.

Ry removed his fingers, and Jed let out a groan.

"There'll be something there soon enough, and then let's see if you groan or scream."

The tip of a toy touched Jed's ass. Disappointment coursed through him. He was expecting Ry's hot cock, not a toy cooled with lube.

Ry pushed the tip in, then pulled it back, and pushed again. The tip of the toy penetrated, but wait a second… Another bulbous head stretched his sphincter muscles before slipping through. Only to be followed by another. The head popped in, then another ribbed portion stretched him. "What the hell do you have?"

"A new toy," Ry said with a bit of laughter in his voice. "Remember that nice, black, ribbed vibe we ordered a couple months ago?"

Jed let out a moan. Oh yeah, he remembered it. Fuck. Ry rubbed his ass cheeks as he continued to push the toy until it was fully inserted.

Jed's dick was rock hard in the cock sleeve, and the

toy up his ass made him want to squirm and buck, but he knew better. If he started pumping his hips in any manner, Ry would deny him the orgasm he desired. And Jed didn't want to jack off in the shower. He wanted Ry to relieve him with his special brand of dominance. He needed it.

Vibrations started low in his ass. Jed let out a breath, then drew it in sharply when the sleeve on his cock began to suck and tighten. "Shit," Jed said.

"Did I forget to tell you that I put the stroker on your cock?" There was laughter in Ry's voice, and Jed gritted his teeth. "The stroker is going to suck your cock. And the vibe in your ass will vibrate to my commands."

If he could have moved, Jed would have jerked out of the stocks, but he couldn't. He was stuck, and he was the one who put himself in this position, knowing just how devious Ry could be. He could always safeword, but what was the fun in doing that? He'd take whatever Ry could dish out and make his Sir proud.

"Is that all you have?" he taunted Ry. A foolish thing to do, but they both needed to let off steam after playing with Katie.

"I have more." Both toys were turned up in intensity, and Jed heard a whoosh of air and then felt the sharp thud of the flogger against his ass.

He cried out, more in surprise than pain. "Fuck."

"How many strokes shall I give you?" Another thud went across his ass, sending a shot of pleasure directly to his balls. The flogger itself landed more of a thud than a sting, but it made him shiver with anticipation.

Heat spread from his ass, to his back and then around to his chest. He wouldn't last too long, not with both his cock and ass being stimulated, and with Ry flogging him… Another thud and the toys were turned up again.

"I love flogging your ass. I can't wait to flog you while you fuck Katie," Ry said as the tails struck his right ass cheek. Ry had been switching from left ass cheek to right and back to left. "Your ass is starting to sway. Are you getting close?"

Close? Hell, Jed was on the verge of climax, but he fought back. He wouldn't come. Not yet. The toys were turned up again; Jet let out another groan. His cock swelled, and his ass tightened around the toy. It all felt so damn good, so damn right. And he wanted more. He needed more. He needed Ry's mastery.

Several more thuddy hits and Jed arched his back, pushing his ass farther into the air. His balls were tight, and it wouldn't take much more to push him over the edge. But he wanted to wait until Ry was done with him before he came.

"Ready for more?" Ry asked.

More? What more could there be?

The toys were turned on full. Painful pleasure streaked up and down from his balls to his toes, making him catch his breath. "Shit."

Ry struck him two more times with the flogger. The last stroke landed right on the vibe in his ass, and Jed screamed as his orgasm ripped through him. He shot his load into the sleeve.

"Yes. Fuck me, Sir. Take your sub. Thrash me, I can take it." The words tumbled from his lips as his hips pumped, the stroker milking his cock. The toy's vibrations slowed until they stopped. Then the vibe in his ass was turned off. Jed lay in the stocks, trying to get control of his breathing. Ry groaned, and sticky warmth shot over Jed's back and ass. Heavy breathing filled the room for several minutes.

"You are so vocal when you come, and I love it." Ry pulled the vibe out, removed the stroker from his cock, and slid the shelf back into place.

Jed lay limp in the stocks, still trying to catch his breath. His ass burned, but his cock was sated for the moment. A warm washcloth swept over his back and ass. A cap popping had him jerking his head up. No, Ry couldn't think of fucking his ass now.

Jed was too on edge and wouldn't be able to handle it. He opened his mouth to shout out his safe word when Ry's palms began caressing his ass cheeks.

"Your ass is red, and there are a few welts from the flogging."

Jed's muscles relaxed as Ry lovingly stroked the cream into his skin. When he was finished, the stock was lifted. Jed rolled his shoulders as Ry rubbed his legs and thighs before helping him to his feet.

Jed pulled Ry into a hug, enjoying the heat of Ry's skin against his. "I needed that. Thank you, my Sir."

"You are the perfect sub, Jed." Ry's arms tightened around him. "I appreciate your submission." Ry took a step back. "How about we shower and then call it a night."

"Fine with me." Jed stretched. "Besides, I'm sweaty, and so are you." He took several steps then glanced over his shoulder. Ry stood by the stocks with a pensive look on his face.

Jed strode over to Ry. "You didn't do anything I didn't want." He clasped Ry on the shoulder.

"I lost control."

"You didn't."

"Jed, your ass was bright red. I raised welts. You're going to be sore."

Jed tightened his fingers on Ry's shoulder. They'd

had this conversation before. "You're a Dominant, Ry; we both know that. You get a little forceful, but you never go over the limit."

"I don't want to get carried away with Katie. She's not ready for that level."

"You won't. I'm here to help you, remember?" He slipped his arm round Ry's shoulders. "Let the past go; you're no longer that out-of-control teenager." Jed maneuvered Ry to the door.

"I need to clean up down here."

"I'll do it. Go get in the shower, and I'll join you shortly." For once, Ry didn't argue with him, which told Jed just how much Ry was in his own head right now. And that wasn't always a good thing.

Once, just once, Ry had gotten carried away with the flogger with Jed. He hadn't injured Jed eight years ago. He'd only caused some discomfort, but nothing that required medical attention. All these years later, Ry was still paying the price. Jed had tried before to get Ry to understand he liked it when they played a little on the edge of pain and pleasure. When dominant Ry really let go. But Ry was afraid of hurting him, of causing him injury.

Now he just had to get Ry to understand he didn't mind. An argument for another day. Jed cleaned up the equipment and headed upstairs. He slipped into the shower behind Ry and pulled the big man to him so Ry's back pressed against Jed's chest. And Ry let Jed hold him until the water was cold and even after they climbed into bed.

Chapter 7

Katie sat in her car the next night, staring out the windshield. She still had a full ten minutes before she needed to be inside the house and in the dungeon. She squirmed in her seat.

"Damn." The word slipped past her lips as her pussy twitched from her movement. She'd been swearing off and on all day, thanks to those balls in her pussy. Even sleeping last night had been a pain. Well, not real pain, but pleasurable pain.

And she still wasn't sure how she felt about following Ry's and Jed's commands. In the bedroom, yes, but her wearing toys outside of their playtime? She hadn't expected it, yet she hadn't said her safe word. Confusion filled her. Logic said nothing outside the bedroom or the dungeon, but her heart wanted to make Ry and Jed proud of her.

Ry had mentioned training, and it wasn't a foreign concept to her. She understood about sub training from Pam and her classes and later had seen it in some of the clubs she'd visited. But until Ry mentioned it last night, she hadn't even thought about it for herself.

Even with the toy inside her and keeping her on edge, she'd visited several office spaces today to see how they would work for her accounting business. It had taken all her willpower to walk around the offices, checking everything out. The balls rubbed up against her pussy walls, making her clit tingle.

She had refrained from calling either Ry or Jed. They'd known darn well what those balls were going to do to her. Heck, she'd bet her next paycheck they had expected another call from her.

A sigh escaped. There wouldn't be a next paycheck unless she found office space. What she'd seen today was a little out of her financial reach right now. She'd have to figure something out soon, because sitting in Gran's kitchen was not exactly the best way to attract clients.

Glancing at her watch, she had five minutes left. No time like the present. Scooping her purse and keys up, she carefully climbed out of her car and slowly walked to the front door. A note was stuck to the thick oak.

"The door is open. We'll make sure you have a key tonight before you leave."

Turning the handle, she pushed the door open and stepped in, listening. Nothing. The house was silent. Katie closed the door and locked it before setting her purse and keys down on the foyer table. She made her way to the dungeon.

After punching in the code, she descended the stairs, each step carefully measured so as not to lose control of the balls inside her. Once in the dungeon, she crossed over to the bed. Tonight, they had put out an outfit. Buck up. She wanted them to know they weren't making a mistake with her. She shook her head. Enough negative talk.

She shed her clothes and put them away before going into the bathroom. She climbed into the shower and pulled the clear plastic curtain. Well, they warned her there wouldn't be privacy there. She twisted the knobs, turning on the water, then she went through the routine Ry and Jed had instructed. She cursed when the balls almost slipped out of her. If she wasn't a submissive, payback would be a bitch. After drying off, she padded back to the bed and picked up the laid-out clothing.

"Shit," she whispered. This wasn't clothing; she might as well be naked. She closed her eyes for a moment, praying for patience. She slipped the panties on, wincing as the balls within her pussy shifted together from one side to the other. There was no crotch, only lace that went around her legs and her waist. The bra wasn't much more concealing as her nipples and breasts were totally bare.

She bit her lip. All part of the training, she reminded herself. She strode over to the mat and took her position. Arms behind her back, legs apart, and staring straight ahead at the wall. It wasn't easy, keeping those balls in her core with her legs apart. She kept tightening her pussy muscles to keep them in, grateful now for all those Kegel exercises Pam encouraged her to do.

The sound of the door opening had her stiffening. The tell-tale footsteps down the stairs, then quiet as they stepped onto the padded flooring. Katie breathed through her nose and out her mouth, trying not only to calm her racing heart, but to keep from demanding they take the balls out.

"Good job today, Kitty Kat," Jed said, walking in front of her.

"God, you're beautiful, sweetheart." Ry joined him.

Her gaze darted from Ry to Jed and then lowered to their erect cocks. They'd undressed before coming to the dungeon. Her gaze slid up taking in their sculpted abs, their bare chests, and finally to their faces. Oh man, they were ready to go. And so was she.

"How many times did the balls fall out today?" Ry asked.

"Twice, Sir Ry."

His eyebrows rose. "Only twice?"

"Yes, Sir Ry." She fought not to shift from one foot to the other, not only because the balls would shift and it would disappoint her Sirs, but because it wasn't going to take much to make her orgasm.

"And how many times did you come today, Kitty Kat?"

Katie bit her lip as her face grew warm. "Five times, Sir Jed." She cursed each time her body took over. And she cursed them for being so diabolical.

Grins broke out on the men's faces, and Katie's heart leapt. Oh, they were planning something for her all right.

"And what did we tell you not to do?" Ry asked.

"You told me not to come, Sir Ry."

"Did you masturbate?" Jed asked.

"No, Sir Jed. The balls caused each climax I had."

Oh, but how she wanted to touch herself, to rub her clit, to make herself orgasm, if only to relieve the pressure building in her pussy, but she hadn't. Not that it mattered, because each time she climaxed, the want, the need, only got worse.

The men looked at each other then back at her, Jed stepped in front of her. He took her by the arms and walked her backward until her butt hit what felt like a padded table, and he moved behind her.

Ry took position in front of her, grasping her waist and lifting her. Jed's arms came around, sliding under her legs with his palms on her thighs, and he pulled her legs apart. Katie had to lean against Jed, or she'd fall. Her pussy was on display for Ry.

"Her pussy is nice and rosy, Jed." Ry stepped closer until she could feel his body heat. "And smells delicious."

Ry slipped two fingers into her wet pussy, and Katie

squealed. Oh, God, her pussy contracted around his fingers. If he moved them just right or touched her clit, she was going to climax again.

She tried to keep still, but her hips shifted up, trying to get pressure on her clit. Ry frowned, and his fingers curled within her pussy. The balls popped out into his palm, making a clanking sound. Ry removed his fingers, and Katie breathed a sigh of relief.

"Your clit is red and inflamed, Katie. I think it needs some relief." Ry lowered his head.

"No, Ry," she yelled before she thought better of it.

Ry's head jerked up, and Jed tightened his arms on her legs.

"Did you just tell me no, my little subbie?" Ry straightened and took a step back.

"Yes, Sir Ry. I'm sorry." Damn, how could she have made such a stupid mistake?

"Well, Jed, what shall we do with this disobedient subbie?"

"Let's put her in the bondage chair, not only for telling you no, but for her unauthorized climaxes today," Jed suggested.

"Not the bondage chair." Ry rubbed his chin, while staring at her.

"Fucking stool?"

"That would be more pleasure than punishment."

Katie ground her teeth together as they talked about her punishment as if she wasn't even there. It was their fault she had spoken out.

"What about the exposure bench?"

"Perfect." Jed released her legs, and her back slid down his body until her feet hit the floor. Ry stood in front of her; his arms curled around her waist, lifting her into his arms. Her heart jumped a beat as he crossed the room before Jed joined them.

Ry set her down on the padded bench. Katie swallowed. She had a feeling she wasn't going to like this, but she wasn't about to say her safe word, either. This couldn't be as bad as having those damn balls in her pussy for twenty-four hours.

"Lay on your back. Jed and I will do the rest."

"Yes, Sir Ry," she whispered, not liking the leather cuffs dangling in Jed's hands. Katie let the cool leather of the bench touch her back. She watched them and waited.

Jed handed Ry a small cuff, and together they secured her wrists. Then they bent down and clipped her arms down toward the floor. She could handle having her arms immobile. When they straightened, Jed handed Ry two more cuffs, one much larger than the other but with chains attached. Her heart sped up.

Ry took her left leg in his hand, cradling it in the nook of his arm. Jed did the same with her right leg. Cuffs were applied to her ankles and right above her knees. Then they raised her legs, keeping them spread as they began attaching the chains to the bench's crossbar.

The cool air caressed her pussy lips. Oh, shit, she was wide open for whatever they wanted to do. Katie concentrated on her breathing as her stomach quivered with unease. They wouldn't hurt her, she reminded herself, but it didn't stop the apprehension dancing along her nerves.

Ry turned and strode across the room while Jed cupped her chin, turning her face to him. "If your legs or arms start falling asleep, let us know immediately."

"Yes, Sir Jed."

"Now, for this next part, we want you to only feel."

Jed placed a blindfold over her eyes and slid the elastic strap behind her head.

She hadn't expected this. At least not this soon. The darkness encompassed her. Oh God, she couldn't do this. She began pulling at the restraints. "Yellow."

"Katie." Ry's voice was right next to her ear. "What is it?"

She fought to breathe. "Blindfold."

"Easy," Jed whispered in her other ear. "We're right here." Fingers brushed against her cheeks. "Breathe, Kitty Kat."

Katie took a deep breath and let it out, trying to quell the panic.

"That's it," Jed said. "Do it again."

"You're perfectly safe, little one," Ry said, his fingers caressed her neck and shoulder.

"He's right." Jed stroked her cheek again.

Her breathing got easier, and her muscles slowly unclenched as they talked softly to her and touched her. It was just them in the room, no one else.

"What scares you?" Ry asked, his fingers massaging her arm in the restraints.

"I…" How could she tell them? This was something no one knew about, not even her grandmother.

"You can tell us," Jed whispered.

"I can't talk like this." She couldn't. She wanted to see their faces when she spoke about what happened. To know they didn't take her fear lightly.

Ry and Jed released the restraints and helped her sit up before the blindfold was removed. Katie blinked several times.

Jed scooped her up and they walked across the room to the bed. Ry sat and Jed set her next to Ry before he sat beside her. Jed slipped his arm around her shoulders while Ry's arm encircled her waist.

"Tell us," Ry said. It was a gentle command, but a command all the same.

"It happened when I was nine." A shiver dashed up her spine. She really didn't want to remember, but they needed to know. "I don't know if you two remember the horrible storm we had that spring."

Jed's lips brushed her temple. "I do. Lots of thunder and lightning." He glanced over at Ry. "Remember the lightning struck the old barn, and we were all out there making sure the fire was out."

"Yes," Ry said.

Another shiver hit her.

"What happened, little one?" Ry squeezed her waist.

"Mom and Grandma were both out." Her voice trembled. You'd think by now that she'd be over this, but there was something about it she couldn't get past. "The storm started, and I hated storms. I went up to my room and curled up in my bed, hoping it would pass quickly."

"And if I remember, it didn't," Ry said, his arms giving her a squeeze.

"No." She closed her eyes, trying to force back the fear. "And then the power went out."

Their arms tightened around her, trying to give her comfort while encouraging her to continue.

"It was so dark I couldn't see anything. I crept out of bed, carefully making my way to the door. I figured if I could find my mom's room, I could find the flashlight." Her breath hitched. She'd been so scared, so alone.

"You're safe, baby," Jed whispered.

"I'd just gotten into the hallway when I heard a noise." She'd frozen in place, afraid to move. Afraid of the noise.

Her heart raced with renewed fear. "Then I heard footsteps. I didn't know what to do."

Ry and Jed moved together, maneuvering her and themselves up the bed, propping her up with pillows against the headboard. Their faces held concern as they sat on each side. Each picked up one of her hands.

"I was so afraid," she whispered. "It was so dark, and there was someone in the house. I wanted to call out but was afraid it wasn't Mom or Gran." Her stomach roiled as the fear coiled there.

"The bottom stair creaked." She couldn't stop the quiver in her voice. "I somehow scooted back into my room, but the steps were coming closer." Tears filled her eyes.

"Fuck," Ry whispered.

"How could we have not known this?" Jed asked.

"Because no one knows," Katie whispered.

"What do you mean, no one knows?" Ry asked.

"I was trying to find the closet when the lights flickered back on." Her voice was a bit steadier now. "I saw a shadow outside my room." She fought against the fear.

"Who was it?" Jed asked softly.

"I don't know. The lights flickered, and all went dark again. But I knew where my closet was. I grabbed my teddy bear and quietly went into the closet."

The next thing she knew, she was being lifted into Ry's lap. Jed cuddled up against her back. Their loving embrace soothed her fears.

"You're safe, little one," Ry whispered, his fingers wiping away the tears on her cheeks.

"We're here for you, Kitty Kat." Jed rubbed her shoulders.

"I don't know how long I sat in the closet, curled up in the back, trying to be quiet. So afraid." She burrowed closer to Ry's chest. "Mom found me after calling my name several times."

"Why didn't they call the sheriff?" Ry asked.

Katie gave a half-laugh with a hiccup. "Because there was no sign of anyone ever getting into the house." She sniffled. "Mom thought it was just my imagination. But I knew someone had been there."

"Of course you did." Jed hugged her.

"I can't stand total darkness. I still sleep with a night light on."

"I'm so glad you told us." Ry kissed her temple.

"Why didn't you say something when you saw the blindfold in my hand?" Jed asked.

"I didn't think it would be so bad." She sniffled. "Then I panicked."

"We hit a silent trigger," Ry said.

Jed leaned back, grabbed the tissue box, and pulled several out before handing them to Ry.

"What's that?" She scrunched up her nose, trying to figure out what they were talking about, but at least the knots in her stomach were slowly going away.

"It's something buried in the psyche that you aren't conscious of, or you would have told us."

"It's okay, sweetie." Jed put his hand under her chin and lifted her face.

Ry used two tissues to remove all traces of her tears. Then he held a new tissue up to her nose. "Blow," he said.

Her cheeks flushed, but she did as he instructed. Ry disposed of the tissues in the bedside bin before gazing down into Katie's face.

"Thank you for trusting us with your fear."

"But you know we're still going to punish you for talking back and for the unauthorized orgasms," Jed informed her.

Her body shook, but it was more from anticipation than fear now.

"Do you think you can keep your eyes closed while we play with you" Ry asked.

"I'm willing to try." The hesitation in her voice made her wince.

"If it bothers you too much, say red. This is why we have safe words."

She nodded.

"Jed's right. We will always respect your usage of safe words." Ry scooted to the edge of the bed and stood with Katie in his arms. He carried her back to the bench.

Within minutes they had her fully restrained. "Okay?"

"Yes, Sir Jed.

"Close your eyes." Katie inhaled sharply. She didn't panic. Maybe talking about it had helped. It didn't mean she was totally comfortable with her loss of sight, but she could rely on her hearing. Besides, she knew who was in the room with her.

"Here we go, subbie," Ry said.

Her breasts were enveloped by warm mouths, and she resisted the urge to open her eyes. Ry and Jed, she reminded herself. Their tongues toyed with her nipples, licking and sucking until they were completely hard and aching.

She moaned in protest when they lifted their heads and cold air made her nipples tighten more.

"So beautiful," Jed murmured.

"Our beautiful subbie," Ry said before he pinched her nipple.

Cold metal closed over her nipple, and she let out a small squeak.

"Easy, little one," Ry said. "It's just nipple clamps."

She ground her teeth together when they clamped her second nipple. She began panting. The clamps weren't too tight, but they caused a straight line of fire from her nipples to her clit. Two pairs of hands caressed her navel, moving south. She sucked in her belly.

What were they planning? She shook her head from side to side, fighting not to open her eyes. She tugged at her wrists. Damn. She never minded when Pam had tied her up to show her what it was like. The good doctor wasn't Ry and Jed.

They turned her on like no other man or men ever could. With her legs chained up as they were, her pussy was open to them. Having on the crotchless panties didn't help.

"Our pussy is wet, Jed."

"Yes, Ry, it is. Very wet."

Her pussy clenched, anticipating…something. She listened for any movement but didn't hear anything.

"For being a disobedient subbie…" Ry said. "You need to be punished."

"And we've decided that your punishments should also be filled with pleasure," Jed said.

Katie was still getting the word *punishments*, plural, through her brain, when she heard a buzzing sound. A vibrator?

"For coming without permission today, you will orgasm twice. Once for each of us," Ry said. "And then you will scream out your third climax for me for telling me no."

Three times? They wanted her to come three times?

Right now?

The buzzing sound came closer. Fingers spread her pussy lips, and Katie braced herself.

"Ahh," she cried as a vibrating bullet touched her clit.

Oh, shit. With it teasing her clit, she wasn't going to last long. Her body had fully calmed down during their talk, but it was ramping up rather quickly with their caresses and the clamps.

Already, the pulses from the bullet coursed from her clit to her core, causing it to tighten. Tingles of pleasure drifted to her lower regions. The tip of the bullet circled around her clit and then over it. She cried out again, straining against the restraints.

"Do you want this, baby?" Jed asked.

"No." She didn't want to be punished, and that was the truth.

"Stubborn Kitty Kat," Jed said. The bullet was placed directly on her clit, and at the same time, they removed the nipple clamps and replaced them with their mouths.

"Fuck," Katie yelled as her orgasm swept over her from head to toe. Her arms jerked at the restraints.

"There's one for me," Jed said, lifting his head and removing the bullet from her clit.

Oh, thank God. Katie lay there panting, her pussy twitching, not sure if her body could take another climax like that.

"My turn," Ry said.

His mouth covered her pussy and clit. His tongue swept over her hard nub and licked into her opening, then lapped back to her clit once again. He alternated between tonguing her pussy and clit.

Katie began shaking her head back and forth as the shudders began. Damn, the man had a talented tongue and lips. The trembling started in her stomach, fluttering down to her clit and pussy.

Oh, God, she wanted to move her hips so bad, to take her hands and tangle them in his hair. But she couldn't. She tugged again and again at the restraints, but they wouldn't give. The flutters grew stronger and stronger.

Ry lifted his head, and Katie cried out, "No, please, Sir Ry." He couldn't stop now.

A male chuckle reached her ears. Ry plunged two fingers into her wet pussy, and she let out a whimper.

"Come for me, my Katie. Come all over my hand. Let me feel your sweet little pussy tighten around my fingers."

Ry pumped his fingers in and out of her wetness as his lips covered her clit again. She moaned when he began sucking her clit and using his tongue to flick it. His fingers never stopped thrusting within her pussy.

It was too much, the touch of his tongue and the feel of his fingers.

The flutters changed to clenching, until… Her neck arched as her pussy clamped down on Ry's fingers, and her climax rolled over her. Her mouth opened, and only a groan came out.

Katie panted, trying to catch her breath. She'd had two orgasms close together, but how could she have another? She could barely think, and her body ached. Her clit pulsed more now than it had all day with the balls lodged inside her pussy. Ry withdrew his fingers. Her channel tightened as if looking for something to hold on to.

"That one was mine," Ry said.

Hands caressed her arms and legs. "Okay?" Jed asked.

"Yes, Sir Jed." She started to open her eyes but shut them before she saw more than a sliver of light. They trusted her. But these two men made her forget everything.

"Good. You have one more climax to give us, and on this one, we want you to scream. Let us hear your pleasure, Katie. Your pleasure is our pleasure," Ry said.

She was about to tell them she didn't have another climax in her when a phallic-shaped object was slipped into her pussy, and at the same time, another round shape touched her clit. She waited, but nothing happened.

"Let me tell you about this little toy," Jed explained. "You've heard of the pleasure wand?"

"Yes, Sir." Oh, God, they had a wand. She'd never tried one of them, but she'd seen them used. Usually, it was just a big round intense vibrating head used on the clit. However, this didn't feel like one.

"We've done something special to this one."

The wand was turned on, and Katie squealed. Not only did the small cock in her pussy pulse, but so did the round shape against her clit. Wetness seeped from her channel.

"We put a rabbit attachment on the wand," Ry said. "Do you know what the rabbit is?"

Katie nodded, her mouth open to gulp air.

"Tell us." Ry slapped her ass, and her pussy creamed.

"It's usually a vibrator with a cock that fits into my pussy, then there is a little rabbit sitting right above the cock and that teases my clit." Just like the one they had on her right now. Her breath caught in her throat. But wait, they said it was a pleasure wand. Oh, fuck, what had these two done?

"Very good." Ry's hand caressed her ass. "But you see, we've modified the wand's speeds, and right now, we're on slow."

If this was slow, she was going to die from the pleasure. Palms covered her breasts, playing with her nipples and pinching them as the wand was turned up.

"Oh, God." Katie struggled in her bonds. The vibrations from the wand were incredible. Her pussy clenched against the fake cock, and the vibrations grew stronger while fingers tweaked her hard nipples.

Panting, Katie tried to fight the rising tide, but the deep rumbling from the wand was no match for her. Her clit twitched and throbbed with each vibration. Her pussy clenched harder and harder, and her spine began tingling.

"Don't fight it," Jed whispered in her ear.

Her head thrashed from side to side. No, she couldn't come again. Yet it was building inside her, hotter than anything she'd ever experienced. Her body was no longer her own. A palm caressed her stomach then slipped down, pressing right above her groin.

The wand was turned on high, and Katie screamed as her climax rolled through her, shaking her from head to toe. The chains shook with her thrashing.

"So fucking beautiful." Ry turned the wand off.

Katie went limp in her bonds, her body sated and her mind mush. She wouldn't be able to move for a month.

* * * *

Jed was proud of Katie for taking her punishment and pleasure, but her lack of movement concerned him. While Katie's breathing was rapid, she didn't appear to be in distress, but Jed wasn't as good at reading the signals as Ry was. Was he failing as one of Katie's Sirs? He glanced at Ry.

"Restraints." Ry's voice was strained. Together, they began releasing her bonds, rubbing her arms and legs, making sure the circulation returned. All the time, Katie didn't say a word, her breathing heavy.

"She hasn't moved," Jed said, worried they'd pushed too far.

"She is totally boneless and sated." Ry lifted Katie into his arms and marched across to the bed. "But her breathing has slowed, and she's smiling."

Jed climbed onto the mattress as Ry lay Katie down, before Ry moved to the bathroom. Brushing her hair off her face, Jed traced her cheek with his finger. "You did so well, Kitty Kat."

"Very well," Ry said, returning to the bed with two washcloths and a bath towel.

Another grin flittered across her lips. The constriction in Jed's chest eased.

Jed took the offered washcloth and began bathing Katie's face, arms, chest, and stomach. Ry started at her feet, continued up her legs, bathed her swollen pussy, and met Jed at her stomach. And Katie never moved or made a sound.

"Did we push too far?" Jed asked.

"Her breathing has returned to normal." Ry used the towel to dry her off. "Her pussy is swollen, but that's to be expected. We played hard, and I suspect she's hit subspace with those smiles she's been giving us."

"Then why hasn't she moved or made any sound at all?"

Ry shrugged his shoulders, but there was concern in his gaze. "Some subs don't. Let's just give her some time." Ry threw the towel and washcloths into the bathroom and joined him and Katie.

Jed snagged the blanket that lay at the end of the bed, pulling it up as he and Ry cuddled up to Katie.

"Time to open those pretty eyes, Katie," Ry said, right next to her ear.

"Mmm." She snuggled closer to them. "I'm fine. I just feel so good. I want to sleep."

Ry chuckled.

Jed let out a breath, relief filling him. "She's okay."

"Yes." Ry brushed Katie's cheek with his finger. "Rest for a bit."

Katie snuggled between them and emitted a soft snore.

"What time is it?" Jed asked.

"Almost nine," Ry said, glancing at his watch. "We need to figure out a better time for this."

"Yeah." Jed patted his stomach as it rumbled. "Maybe we should keep the hard play until the weekends and keep it a bit lighter on weeknights."

"We haven't been that hard on her."

"No, but it's taking a toll on all of us." Jed rubbed his chin. "We all have to work." His stomach rumbled. "Plus we ate a light dinner, and it's not good to eat this late at night."

"We need her here earlier."

"Ry, we can't take up all her time. She does have her grandmother and, apparently, a job."

"What job?"

"Jason said he saw Katie in town today, looking at real estate. When he asked her about it, she told him she was looking for office space for her accounting business."

"Aww, hell." Ry drew his hand through his hair. "I've been so damn focused on keeping her with us, I never thought of what she might need."

"Me, either. We're not being very good Sirs, are we?" Jed wasn't going to let Ry take all the blame himself.

"No, and I know better."

"We really need to make this about more than sex. Why don't we take the next few nights to talk about our lives?"

"Hell, yes, it's more than just sex."

"Then let's show her that. We need to show Katie our lives so she'll let us in on hers. Hell, we still don't know why she left New York City and came back home."

"Damn, I've been doing this all wrong." Ry shook his head.

"No." Jed touched Ry's arm when he would have gotten out of bed. "You went into Dom mode from the second you saw Katie, and you've stayed. There is nothing wrong with it, so stop blaming yourself."

Ry brushed his hand over his chest. "I can't lose her again. We can't."

"We won't." Jed wasn't about to let Katie go any more than Ry was, but they needed to be smart about this. "Let's take it down a notch, see how she reacts."

"Agreed." Ry lay down, his head cradled on his arm, his other hand resting on Katie's stomach.

"Tomorrow we start anew," Jed said, settling against the pillows, the tips of his fingers touching Ry's where they rested on Katie's belly.

Chapter 8

The next morning, Katie woke in her own bed, stretched, and then winced as her sore muscles protested. Ry and Jed had given her quite a workout last night, but she'd enjoyed every second of it. Well, almost every second. Her panic over the blindfold had been the only downside of the night. But they'd both been so understanding of her fear. She glanced at her open bedroom door and let out a shaky breath. She was still off-balance just remembering that night.

Slipping out of bed, she padded nude to the bathroom and turned the shower on.

After a few minutes, she stepped in and sighed. The hot water caressed her skin, helping her sore shoulder muscles relax. Katie stood there, letting the water slide down her body before picking up the shampoo bottle and pouring some out.

She wondered what Ry and Jed had planned for tonight. She'd been a little embarrassed she'd fallen asleep on them last night. But after three orgasms, her body needed the rest.

She'd woken around eleven to find the men on each side of her, their hands resting on her stomach, both sound asleep. She had taken a few minutes to study them. Ry, with his raven hair mussed and his jaw relaxed for once. Always in charge, always the one to take control. Asleep he looked almost angelic, and she was hard-pressed not to caress his face to show him control was overrated.

Then there was Jed. His dark brown hair, longer than Ry's but just as silky. When he was awake, his blue eyes always twinkled with mischief. He was gentler than Ry, but he also liked to take control at times. It was no wonder these two were as close as any two men could be. They'd grown up and lived together after Jed's mother died. They were more than friends—partners in crime and all hers.

"Katie," her grandmother yelled through the bathroom door. "Breakfast in ten minutes."

"Okay, thanks." Katie washed the soap out of her hair and turned off the shower. Her grandmother had been awake when she arrived home last night. But all she did was smile and tell Katie to sleep well.

After drying off, she dressed. Her leg muscles protested as she went down the stairs, but the smell of coffee and pancakes—along with a growling stomach— urged her on.

"Gran, breakfast smells delicious." Katie poured herself a cup of coffee and then kissed her grandmother's cheek.

"Well, you're going to need your strength."

Katie's coffee cup hit the table with a thunk, and she stared at her grandmother. "Wh—what makes you say that?" Oh damn, what did her grandmother know?

"Oh, sit down." Gran waved her hand, and Katie sat before her knees gave out. Gran set a pile of pancakes in front of her. "Now, eat them all, and we'll talk."

Crap. How was she going to eat now? But her stomach rumbled, reminding her she hadn't eaten since dinner last night, and even then, she hadn't eaten much. Grabbing the syrup, she slathered it on her pancakes and dug in.

The real maple syrup made her groan around a forkful. It had been a long time since she'd had real syrup, and if she wasn't careful, she'd gain weight. Time to start exercising again. Not that she wasn't getting enough exercise with Ry and Jed.

Heat flooded her veins, and she glanced at her grandmother. How much did she know? Or was she making educated guesses? Katie finished her breakfast, stood up, put her plate in the sink, and got another mug of coffee. Somehow, she figured she might need it.

Her grandmother sat back in her chair, staring at her, and Katie fought not so squirm. "Okay, out with it, Gran."

"Ry and Jed."

Katie started to choke. Gran stood, but Katie waved her back down. Wheezing, she stared across the table. "What about them?" she squeaked out.

"Those two boys have grown even closer since you left, Katie. They were both heartbroken when you went to New York City without a word."

What could she say to that? She had left them and chased after a dream she could never achieve. "I've apologized to them."

"That's a start. I know why you went to New York with your father." Gran's lips pursed as if she tasted something sour. "And while you haven't told me why you came home, I can guess."

"Gran, it just didn't work out." She almost winced at the sweetness of her own voice. Truth be told, Randall was as bad as her gran sensed, but he was still her father.

"That's all water under the bridge. I just want you to know that Ry and Jed won't take your defection in stride this time. They'll come after you."

Katie shifted in her chair. What did Gran know? "Umm, Gran…"

"Katie, I know all about those boys and their parents.

No business of mine. But those two are now men and not the boys you remember." Gran fanned her face with her fingers. "Don't make the mistake and think you can wind them around your little finger like you used to."

"No kidding." She burst out laughing at the grin on Gran's face.

"Aren't you concerned that I'm with both of them?" Katie's voice shook a little, but she had to ask.

"No." Gran patted her gray hair before she took her plate and cup to the sink. "Those two love each other." Gran faced Katie. "I'm aware of their relationship. They'll treat my Katie right or answer to me."

Katie jumped to her feet and enveloped her grandmother in a hug. Gran understood. "Others might make nasty comments."

"Posh. Old biddies if they do. You do what is right for you and your heart. That's all I ask." Gran patted her on the back. "Now, there is one other thing we need to discuss."

"And that is?" She took a step back and eyed her grandmother warily.

"Sheila Reynolds came into the tea shop yesterday."

Katie nodded. Gran had run the tea shop in town since Katie was sixteen; she'd even worked there after school.

"She mentioned you were trying to find some office space."

That was it? Relief poured through her veins. "Yes, Gran. I need to set my accounting business up. I have clients I need to take care of, and I'm sure there are people here in town who could use a good accountant and tax person."

"I think it's wonderful." Gran clapped her hand together. "But you don't need to look for office space. You can use the office here in the house."

Katie blinked. "But Gran, that was Grandpa's office. You haven't touched it since he passed."

"I cleaned it out last year. Papers gathering dust and such. It was time to do it."

"But…"

"Hush, child." Gran waved her hands. "I want you to use it. There's no sense in you spending good money when there's a perfectly good office here."

Her grandmother's face blurred as Katie's eyes filled with tears. Her grandfather had been a math teacher before he retired, which was where Katie got her love for numbers. "Oh, Gran." Katie threw her arms around her grandmother.

"He'd like having you in his office, doing a job you love." Gran patted her arms.

"Thank you, Gran."

"Nothing to thank me for. Now, off with you." Gran sniffled and pushed Katie to arm's length. "I've got to get to the tea shop, and I bet you're eager to go into the office."

"Yes." Katie kissed her grandmother's cheek and made her way across the house to her grandfather's office. She threw open the French doors and sighed.

It still smelled like tobacco and the cheap cologne her grandpa used. The large oak desk needed a good polish, but that was the easy part. She was going to need a good chair, file cabinet, and internet access for her business. While Gran had internet Katie need to have her own.

She'd warned her clients she'd be out of touch, and if it was an emergency, they could call her. Every time her phone rang she'd check the caller ID. If it was her father or ex, she ignored it. If it was a client, she answered it. She'd change her number, but it was one she had before she left Felton's Creek.

Which reminded her that she needed to check her messages. She turned her phone off last night and needed to turn it back on. She deleted six voice mails without even listening to them. The seventh one—from Dr. Pam—caused a smile to crease her lips. She finished with the voice mail, deleted it, and went to her missed calls list.

Chapter 9

Jed slammed his truck door and started up the walkway to Katie's house. Just as he reached the front door, it opened, and Miss Mazie stood there.

"Hello, Jed, dear," Miss Mazie said when she saw him.

He flashed Katie's grandmother a smile. "Morning, Miss Mazie. Is Katie about?"

"Yes. And I'm glad you're here. You can help Katie get the office organized." She held open the door. "Go right in. Down the hallway on your right."

"Thanks." Jed dropped a kiss on Miss Mazie's cheek as he made his way into the house and to the office. Jed halted right outside the office door. He wanted to see how Katie was doing after last night.

"Hello, darling, how are you?" Katie's voice carried outside the room. "Yes, I've missed you too."

Darling? Who the hell was she talking to? Old fears reared their ugly head, going back to a time when women had cheated on him after Katie. Then as he and Ry were finding their feet in their relationship, there had been that woman who tried to play him and Ry off each other. Had Katie left someone behind in New York City? She wasn't the type to lie. But it had been eight years. His chin came up, and he wasn't proud of himself as he listened to her side of the conversation.

"Yes, I'm happy to be home." Katie paused and laughed. "Even if it did mean leaving you. You should come visit."

Jed's fingers curled into fists as he stood outside the door. She was inviting another man to visit her? That was so not going to happen. He stepped into the doorway, but Katie was facing away from him, leaning against the desk.

She gave a husky laugh. "Sure, bring your special kit. I'm sure we could find some use for it."

His temper flared. No fucking way was some man going to… Jed strode over to Katie. He snatched the phone out of her hand and lifted it to his mouth. Katie was his. She held his heart.

"I don't give a fuck who this is, but Katie is taken, now and forever." Jed hit the end button and glared at Katie.

"What the hell are you doing?" She reached for her phone, but he held it out of her reach.

"No other men, Katie. That isn't negotiable."

"I'd assumed that. Now give me my phone."

"Are you going to call him back?"

"Yes."

His temper hit the roof. "Then you can't have it." Jed pocketed the phone as it began to ring.

"Damn it, that could be a client. I need my phone." She held her hand out for it.

Her telling him it could be a client was the only reason he fished the cell out of his pocket. Glancing at the display, he saw the name Pam. Good, it wasn't the man. He handed the phone over to her.

"Hi," Katie said. "Yeah. Sorry about that." She glared at him. "I have a Neanderthal standing in what is to be my new office."

Jed cupped the nape of her neck, giving it a light

squeeze in warning.

Katie glared at him. "Yes. He's the one who hung up on you." She stuck her tongue out at him. Jed couldn't help it. He burst out laughing and released his grip on her.

"Okay, call you later." She hit the end button. "This isn't funny, Jed."

She stood with hands on hips, legs spread, and all he could think about was peeling those jeans down those long legs, taking her panties with them. He'd lick her pussy until she came at least twice, and then he'd fuck her across that big oak desk.

"You know a guy named Pam?" he asked, finally controlling his laugher.

"No, I know a woman named Pam. And don't get off the subject. If you ever do something like that again, I'll twist your balls into shriveled grapes." She punctuated each word with a finger poke to his chest.

"Kitty Kat, you couldn't if you wanted to." He started to reach for her and found himself flat on his back against the hardwood floor, his arms pinned behind his back by his body weight. When his brain caught up with his body, he had to admit he was impressed. Very few women could take him by surprise and pin him down.

Katie straddled his legs and placed her palm right over his balls. "Want to rethink that statement?" she asked.

"What the heck…" Katie's grandmother stood in the doorway her eyes wide. "Oh, sorry. Katie, honey, I'll see you tonight."

Katie groaned. "Gran," she yelled.

"No, it's okay. Have fun." The front door slammed, and Katie rolled her eyes.

"So now that you have me in this position, what do you plan on doing with me?" Jed relaxed his muscles, but his cock stiffened in anticipation.

"Maybe you should learn not to eavesdrop on other people's conversations—or jump to conclusions." She kept the pressure on him so he couldn't buck her off, not that he wanted to try. He liked her straddling his cock.

"Sorry." He tried to make it come out sincerely but knew he failed when her eyes darkened. His heart squeezed with love and passion.

"Sorry, my ass. I should tie you up and whip you for what you just did."

His dick leaped beneath his jeans, pressing hard against the fabric. Oh hell, he couldn't let her do that, but damn if the idea didn't excite him. He'd never let a woman whip him before, but the thought of Katie doing it made his blood boil. He opened his mouth, and his phone rang.

"I really need to get that," he said, shifting his hips.

"Let's just make sure it's not a woman." She slipped his phone out of his pants pocket. She looked at it and smiled before hitting the talk button. "Hi, Ry." She listened. "Jed's a little, shall we say, flat on his back, and about to have his balls turned into grapes."

"Fuck." Jed tried to buck, but Katie leaned over him, pressing a hand to his chest. His hands were trapped beneath the small of his back. In this position, he couldn't get leverage, and she was still sitting on his legs.

"Bye." Katie hit the end button and tossed his phone onto the desk. "Ry said to have fun."

"Bastard." Ry would say that. "Come on, Katie. I really am sorry I jumped to conclusions."

"You just want me to let you up." She rocked her hips against his bulging cock.

"Yes, no… Fuck." Her fingers slipped between their bodies, and she squeezed his cock. Excitement shot up his spine.

"It's bigger than I remember." She stroked him through the denim.

"And getting bigger by the second," he muttered, gritting his teeth against her touch.

"Poor Jed," Katie whispered. Leaning over him once again, her body shifted, her lips inches from his. "All hard and wanting."

"Two can play this game." She'd adjusted her position just enough for him to rock his body, allowing him to free one arm. He grabbed her around the waist, and he flipped her onto her back. Now he was on top. He grabbed her wrists and pinned them above her head with one hand, his hips straddling hers. "Now who has the upper hand?"

Katie's eyes grew wide as Jed began undoing her blouse. "Jed," she started.

"You started it, Kitty Kat, and I'm going to finish it." He pulled her shirt apart. "Thank God for front clasp bras." He flipped the clasp, and her breasts spilled out.

"We're in my grandmother's house," she reminded him.

"Yes, and she left for work." Leaning down, he licked the right nipple then the left before taking the right one in his mouth and biting it.

"Ouch." She squirmed beneath him.

He gave her a grin before biting her left nipple, and this time she only tried to buck him off. But he wasn't going anywhere. "Such pretty pink nipples. I can't wait until I can clamp them again." Jed nuzzled between her breasts. "Just think how that will feel, Kitty Kat. Your nipples in clamps, a chain hanging between them, and my fingers on that chain, pulling it. Making your nipples stretch, making you hot, and making you squirm for more."

Her head moved from side to side. "I don't like pain."

"It won't be pain; it will be pleasure." He licked the underside of her breasts. "And when I pull the clamps off, I'll thrust into your wet pussy so you won't even notice the slight pain of the blood rushing back to them. And you'll come from the pleasure of it all."

Katie's breathing sped up, and Jed fought back a grin. She was turned on, just as he was. Good. Because he was going to turn up the heat more.

"I bet your pussy is wet now." His fingers walked their way down her stomach to the top of her jeans. He paused for a second, then unfastened the button before unzipping them.

"Jed, please," she whispered.

He slipped his palm down over her abdomen and beneath her panties. Heat radiated from her pussy as he pressed one finger inside.

She cried out, tried to raise her hips, but his weight prevented her from doing that.

"Yes, soaking wet." He stroked his finger in and out of her pussy, watching her eyes widen and hearing her breathing increase.

He could make her come right here, right now. His brain finally got enough blood that he realized what he was doing. Fuck. He was violating a hard limit. Withdrawing his finger, he slid it into his mouth, tasting her honey cream. Then he released her arms and climbed off her legs.

"I'm sorry." Jed rose to his feet, reached down and helped her up. She scrambled to button her blouse and jeans. "I lost my head and ignored your hard limit." He dropped his head. Hard limits were sacred, and there was no way he should have forgotten it.

Katie's soft touch on his cheek caused him to raise his head. Concern filled her features. "We both got carried away."

"But it's my responsibility to remember."

"It's also mine to use my safeword. Don't beat yourself up about it. Gran's house being a hard limit has to do more with her catching us than anything else."

"That doesn't make it right I forgot."

Katie shook her head. "Why did you come over anyway?"

"To check on how you were doing after last night. Miss Mazie said you might need help setting your office up." His voice was gruff from his own arousal. He could jack off later or go down to the dungeon and use one of the masturbators. But Katie… She would have to wait since they'd ordered her not to come without their permission.

"She did?" Confusion showed on her face.

Jed placed his fingers under her chin and tilted it up. "Yes. What do you need?"

"A long, hard fuck." Katie closed her eyes. "Damn it, I didn't mean to say that out loud."

Jed snagged her around the waist. "We'll have to wait on that long, hard fuck. But I promise you will have it."

She blew out a breath. "Frustration is thy name." Her gaze drifted to his groin, and his cock pulsed.

Jed slapped her ass, and she jumped. "Concentrate, Katie."

"Yes, boss." She snapped him a salute.

"You got that right. I'm the boss." He grinned at her. "What do you need for the office?" Crisis averted.

"Chair, file cabinet, and internet."

"Let's drive over to Monroe. They've got a good office supply store, and you can get what you need."

"I'll go put on my shoes and get my purse." Katie danced out of the room.

His cell phone rang, and he snatched it off of the desk. "Ry."

"So why did Katie want to damage your balls?"

"I overheard her on the phone and jumped to the conclusion she was talking to a man."

"And was she?" Ry's voice hardened. Past events made them both leery.

"No, and she made it clear she didn't appreciate my, shall we say, jumping to the wrong conclusion."

Ry laughed. "I take it your balls are still intact?"

"Yeah." Jed rubbed the back of his neck. Confession time. "I screwed up."

"How?"

"We're in Miss Mazie's house, and I took advantage of Katie with foreplay. It was a hard limit not to do anything in the house."

"Did you ignore her safe word?"

"No. She didn't say it, but I should have remembered." Jed paced around the office.

"I agree. Is Katie upset?"

"No. She was actually very understanding." In a way that made Jed feel worse.

"We're going to make mistakes Jed. As long as you didn't hurt Katie, and you stopped when you realized what you were doing. I say no harm no foul."

Jed released a breath. "I'll do better."

"Of course you will. What are you doing today?"

Jed's shoulders relaxed. "I'm taking Katie to Monroe to pick her up some office furniture and supplies."

"Good. I'm glad you're there to keep an eye on her."

"Ry, Katie isn't like other women."

"I know." Ry blew out a breath.

"She's coming back now. Talk to you later."

Katie appeared in the doorway. "I'm ready."

"Then let's go." He took her arm and escorted her out to his truck.

* * * *

Four hours later, Ry pulled up to Miss Mazie's house, got out of the SUV, and strolled up to Jed, who was shaking his head. His truck was full to the brim with office furniture and supplies.

"Is this all Katie's?"

"Yep." Jed rubbed his neck.

"Hey, Ry," Katie said as she came out of the house.

"Hi, Katie." Ry snagged her by the waist and gave her a quick kiss before releasing her. God, he loved the feel of her soft lips.

"You didn't have to come over. I could help Jed get this stuff in the house."

"This is man's work," Jed said, puffing his chest out.

Katie laughed, and Ry couldn't help but grin. She was in good spirits today. His gut unclenched a bit. The incident last night didn't seem to be affecting her. That was good. Now he could wonder about all the office supplies. "We don't want you to hurt yourself." Ry leaned over and whispered in her ear, "That's our job."

A blush crept over Katie's cheeks, and Ry glanced at Jed, who had a shit-eating grin on his face.

"Okay, let's get this show on the road," Ry said. "I only have an hour for lunch."

An hour later, everything was unloaded, and the furniture in place except for the office chair. "I'll let Jed put the chair together," Ry said.

"Thanks." Jed gave him the finger.

Ry pulled Katie into his arms. "Dinner tonight at the house, and then we're going to discuss why you're setting up this office."

"Yeah, you mentioned something about clients this morning," Jed said.

"You don't know?" Katie glanced between Jed and him. She wiggled her eyebrows. "Well, it's to start taking reservations for your dungeon, of course. There's a big call for playrooms like yours."

"What?" Jed roared, and Ry laughed. Katie could always make him laugh, and it had been a long time since he felt this good around a woman.

"I'm only teasing." Katie held her hand out to Jed, who took it. "I'm not about to advertise our activities."

Ry's radio went off. "Okay, I'm off. See you both later." One quick kiss on Katie's lips and a pointed look at Jed.

"What was that look about?" Katie asked.

"I don't know what you're talking about." Jed opened the chair box and began unpacking it.

"I'll figure it out."

"You do that," Ry said, striding toward the front door.

The doorbell rang. "Yeah, that's the internet guy." She spun on her heel, ducked around him, and ran ahead of him.

* * * *

Katie settled down on the sofa after dinner that night, waiting for Ry and Jed. She'd had a fun afternoon setting up her office and getting everything into place. She glanced up as both men walked into the room and took their seats on either side of her. Her pulse sped up.

"So, Katie, what are you going to do in this new office of yours?" Ry asked.

Katie smiled. "Well, one of the things I did while I was in New York was become a CPA with a specialty in forensic accounting."

Jed whistled, and Ry shook his head. "You always had a way with numbers," Ry said.

"Yes, and I really enjoy the work." She did. That was one thing her father couldn't take away from her no matter how much he tried.

"And the clients you have?" Jed asked.

"Mainly people I keep books for as a CPA. When I was working for my…" She bit her lip. She really didn't want to bring her father's name up.

"Go on," Ry urged.

"When I was working for my father, I worked in the accounting department. Kind of boring."

"Nothing you do is boring," Jed said.

"Now that we have that out of the way, we need to talk about the past," Ry said. The two men scooted closer to her. "We really should have discussed this before last night. I've been remiss. Did we scare you away when you were eighteen?" Ry asked, his voice low and husky.

Katie shook her head. She wasn't ready to talk about this yet. But… Ry began rubbing the nape of her neck as Jed rubbed her back. Her fears started to lessen.

"We need to understand why you ran, Katie," Jed said.

"Can't it be enough that I'm back?" She closed her eyes against the conflicting sensations of the soothing movements of their hands against her neck and back and her stomach churning with fear she didn't want to acknowledge.

"It won't work if we don't talk about why you left," Ry said.

"It's been working just fine so far. Why aren't we in

the dungeon?" She'd rather be there with them than having this discussion.

"Because we need to talk," Ry said.

"Isn't that a woman's line?" She wanted to pull away from them, but she didn't. Their touch was soothing.

Jed laughed. "It might be, but Ry is right."

Work-rough hands cupped her chin, lifting it. When had she lowered her head? She wanted to hide, but they weren't going to let her.

"Nothing you can say will change anything between us, Katie." Ry feathered his fingers from her temple to her neck.

"Except if you ask us to leave you alone. But based on what has happened already, you want us," Jed said.

"Yes, I want you both." That wasn't hard to admit because she did want them both. Unnatural. The word filtered through her brain and tension seeped back into her bones.

"What happened, Kitty Kat?" Jed whispered in her ear.

She shook her head and bolted off the sofa, away from their touch. "I can't." Katie wrapped her arms around herself. Why couldn't she tell them? They needed to know why she left and why she came back.

Maybe because she blamed herself for her own stupidity in listening to people who wanted nothing more than to use her. Even after she had all the evidence in hand, she still wanted to believe in her father, but as the cliché went, there is one straw that broke the camel's back. That straw came in a form she was still having issues comprehending.

But they were right. She needed to explain what happened, even if it made her look foolish. "The night of my eighteenth birthday was magical." The words spilled from her lips without conscious thought. "You two made sure of it." She paced the floor, trying to contain her nervousness. "We made love that night, the three of us. Oh, maybe not the way you wanted to." Her lips flitted upward. "But it was still us three."

A shiver climbed up her spine as she remembered that night. From the time she was fourteen, she'd had a crush on Ry and Jed. Of course she'd been too young to fully understand the family dynamic. When she turned seventeen, they hung out at her gran's tea shop when she was working. The girls in her high school would hang out there as well, and Katie would overhear them gossiping.

She ignored most of it, especially when they started discussing sex. Then her eighteenth birthday had arrived.

The men had shown up at her party, looking delicious. She'd flirted with them. Then the next night, they snuck into her bedroom. She'd known then she wanted these two. Gran always told her to follow her heart, and her heart had led her to Ry and Jed.

Jed had held her close as Ry took her virginity, and then Ry caressed her as Jed made love to her. They'd been more than gentle with her, and to this day, she still trembled with pleasure.

"The next day you were gone," Ry said, his tone rough.

"Yes." Katie sighed. "I'm not proud of what I did." Hell, she should have faced them and told them the truth. Instead, she had run. She'd let fear of the unknown send her scrambling off with her father.

"Why did you leave?" Jed asked, his voice quiet, almost serene.

"I'd heard the rumors about you two." She shook her

head to displace her father's voice. "About how you shared women. I was frightened."

"Of us?" They asked together.

"No. Of myself." She stopped her pacing and faced them. Hopefully they would understand. "I was eighteen; you two had made love to me just as I'd dreamed about, and then my father showed up with promises of a life with him, in New York City, that I'd only dreamed of."

Ry and Jed moved to stand, and she raised her hands to stop them. She needed them to stay seated and not touch her, or she'd never get this out. "I let my father convince me that I could have a better life at his side. And somehow he knew about you two." And the words he'd used scared her at that time. Now she knew it was just a way to control her.

"What did he say?" Ry's fingers curled into fists.

"That it was unnatural, and that was no way to live." Tears blurred her vision. "Your parents being so close, and how Ry's mom had sex with both Jed's dad and Ry's dad. It wasn't normal. It wasn't how men and women were supposed to be." Now she could see what her father had been doing. She lost eight years because she was too young and naïve to understand. "I was so damned confused. I wanted to stay, and I wanted to go. And…" She took a shaky breath.

"And what?" Jed asked in a quiet voice.

"Peggy Morris." Her voice trembled. Just saying the woman's name made her stomach clench with dread. "My father brought her to talk to me."

Both men swore, and in a way, Katie agreed. Peggy had dated both Ry and Jed. She'd played them off one another, and when they caught on and dumped her, Peggy became quite a bitch. It didn't matter they were all adults.

"She made you afraid," Ry said as he rose and paced to the kitchen and back.

"Yes." Katie raised her head. "Not of the two of you, but of how I felt." She took a step closer to Ry before he paced to the kitchen once again. "I was confused. I wanted to be with you both. Wanted both of you as lovers, and she kept on and on about how it wasn't right. And painful." And her father hadn't helped either.

"I don't get it." Ry raked his hand through his hair. "We would never hurt you."

"Ry." Katie placed her palm on his arm. "She made it sound like being with the two of you would be all pain and humiliation. That I'd never have a life. I would be a slave to the two of you. I would have no voice and would have to obey the two of you no matter what. She made it sound like Ry's mother was a slave to your fathers."

"Fuck, no." Ry curled his arms around Katie, pulling her to him.

"Never." Jed stood and hugged her from the back.

This time, she sank into their embrace, enjoying the warmth and security. She'd gotten the words out. Now she needed them.

"My mom was a strong woman." Ry's breath brushed her cheek.

"She took care of Ry and me. Lord, she was the only mother I remember," Jed said.

"I know." Katie put her hands on Jed's where they rested against her stomach.

"And what did your father say?" Jed asked.

"He convinced me that Peggy was right. While I was still trying to sort things out, he had me packed up and on the road." She closed her eyes against the pain. "He barely let me say goodbye to Gran."

"Why didn't you come talk to us?" Jed rubbed his cheek against hers.

"How could I?" Her gaze captured Ry's. "My father was making things sound so reasonable." The knots in her stomach returned. "And I was afraid they might be right."

Katie tightened her arms around Ry's waist when he would have pulled away from their embrace. The hurt in his eyes was like a dagger to her heart.

"Ry, I was eighteen. All I knew was from what little I had found to read, what Peggy and my father told me. None of it was pretty." She took a deep breath. "The times I met your mom, she was kind to me, but she was always busy doing something around the house or running errands for your fathers. It all sounded so reasonable."

Ry let out a breath before relaxing back into her embrace. "I know, baby."

"So I went to New York City."

"Will you tell us about that?" Jed asked.

She nodded, her heart lighter than it had been in a long time.

"If we're going to do this, let's get comfortable." Ry slipped from her embrace, maneuvered an extra-large love seat into position, and made some adjustments before Jed led her over.

"Why not the sofa?" she asked.

"We can be more comfortable with the reclining love seat," Ry said.

Jed guided her to the middle, and they each took a position on either side of her. "Lean back and relax," Ry said.

Taking a deep breath, Katie did so. The seat reclined, the three of them half lying down. Both men had their arms around her shoulders, and she snuggled up against them.

"There, that's better," Jed said. "Tell us what happened after you left with your father."

"Well, at first, everything was fine. I was living with my father in Manhattan but wanted to get out on my own. In order to do that, I needed a job." She'd been so foolish. "I was chasing a dream where my father actually cared about me."

For the next hour, she told Ry and Jed about her first few years in New York City and how her father hadn't wanted her to work. But Katie didn't like sitting in her father's luxury apartment doing nothing. She began to work for another company, started working her way up the ladder, and began college.

Her father had been furious when he found out about the job and that she wasn't out spending his money or with friends. Friends her father carefully curated. But there hadn't been much he could do about it. She'd moved out into her own place. Yes, it had been small, but she didn't have to answer to anyone. After getting her degree in accounting, the company she worked for promoted her, and she started learning about forensic accounting.

When the economy took a nosedive, the company she had worked for was bought out by a bigger company—her father's. So she ended up working for her father anyway, but at least no one knew the truth.

"It wasn't until a year ago I realized my father had been making some shady deals."

Both men stiffened. "Did you confront him?"

"No." Katie shifted, enjoying the warm cocoon the two men provided her. She was safe here. "My father would have denied it anyway. But there was more to it than that."

Was she ready to go there? Yes, she had to. Ry and

Jed needed to understand why she came back. It was more than her father's broken promises. A lot had to do with her learning about BDSM. She yawned. She wanted nothing more than to take a nap.

"Will you tell us?" Jed asked.

"Yes," she whispered, her lashes drifting shut. "But not tonight." She wiggled around again and let herself drift off. Lord, she was tired.

* * * *

Jed glanced down at Katie and smiled. Her eyes were closed and her breathing deep. Satisfaction at her trust curled around his heart. "She's asleep," Jed whispered.

"Yes. She likes to fall asleep on us." Ry tightened his arm around her. "What do you think about what she said?"

Jed ran his free hand over his face. "Makes sense, but I also feel as if there's something more."

"Me too." Ry brushed a kiss against Katie's temple. "And it has to do with her father."

"Yep. Randall was always an asshole."

"True. But how did he know about us spending the night with Katie and that we'd dated Peggy?"

"I don't know." Jed rubbed his chin.

"Katie trusted her father, and he broke that trust."

Jed sighed. "Do you think she'll tell us the full story?"

"Eventually. Right now, let her rest."

Both men closed their eyes. This was the best place to be right now. Katie was in their arms and their lives.

Chapter 10

Three days later, Katie strode into the barn to find Jed. He'd called earlier and asked her to come over. She gnawed at her lower lip as she sauntered toward the office in back. She stopped to pet several of the horses.

The last couple of days had been trying. The calls from her ex and her father hadn't let up. The other day, she had told her father—again—she wasn't going back to the City and to stop calling. She'd considered changing her cell number, but her father would probably find it.

At least things between her, Ry, and Jed had improved. She'd worried they'd be angry at her explanation of why she left, but both reassured her that while they were upset at the time, now they understood. They hadn't played since her revelations about why she left, but they had cuddled and spent time together. They were slowly building their relationship and their trust in each other.

She sighed and raised her hand to knock on the partially open door. Jed swore and then muttered a few words, causing a grin spread over her face.

"Are you having issues in here?" she asked, pushing the door open and stepping into the office.

"Thank God, you're here." Jed stood up and moved out from behind the desk. "Come figure this out for me." He gestured to the computer, his face tight with tension.

"What are you having problems with?" She shook her head. Jed wasn't one to get frustrated easily. She maneuvered around him and behind the desk.

"Hell if I know. I've been working on this for the past two days, and I'm still stuck."

Katie sat down and stared at his computer screen. She scrolled up and down and sighed. What a disaster. "What exactly are you trying to do?"

"I'm trying to pay the vet, and find out when I last paid for hay and how much. Figure out who owes me money, who I owe money to, and what's left over."

Katie nodded, grabbed a pencil and paper, jotted down some notes, and looked back at the screen. This would take some time. She glanced up at Jed. "Go play with your horses and come back in two hours."

"Ordering me around, are you?"

Katie grinned at him then made a shooing motion with her hand. Jed laughed and strode out of the office, closing the door behind him.

Katie focused on the computer screen. Maybe she could make some sense out of the mess Jed had made. An accountant he wasn't.

Several hours later, Katie stood and stretched. Luckily, she had a flash drive in her purse. She copied his files over. She'd done most of it on paper already, but there was still more to do. She sauntered over to the office door and opened it. Jed stood at the end of the barn, quietly talking to one of the horses. His soft voice melted Katie's heart. He was so good with the animals. Quietly, she walked toward them. She stopped outside the stall as Jed hung up the horse's halter. The horse's ears perked up, and he turned his head and faced her.

"I'm almost done," Jed said. "Why don't you come in

and say hi to Coulter." He held out his hand to her.

She placed her hand in his and let him draw her closer to the stall. The fresh scent of hay tickled her nose.

"This is Coulter," Jed said as she slid closer to them.

"He's beautiful."

"Did you figure out my mistakes?" Jed asked.

"Not completely." She stroked Coulter's brown nose. He was a beautiful horse, brown with big white patches all over his body. "I wrote down what you needed to know and copied your files over onto a flash drive. I'll upload them into my computer and fix everything, if that is okay."

"More than okay. Thank you." Jed shifted behind her, his chest against her back, his arms coming around her body as she stroked the horse. "I want to hire you to do the books."

She tilted her head back to look at him. "You don't need to do that."

"Yes, I do." He dropped a kiss on her nose. "I hate accounting and anything to do with it."

"How did you survive this long without an accountant?"

"I didn't. John Knowles used to do them, but he retired two months ago. I figured I could keep it up, but as you can see, it didn't work out."

"Did someone replace John?" John Knowles retired? Oh, yes, now she remembered looking at his old office space. Maybe it was a good thing she was running an ad in the local paper. She might be able to pick up more business.

"Not that I'm aware of. He did suggest someone over in Monroe, but it does make it difficult for people here." His arms tightened around her waist. "Good thing you're an accountant."

"Yes." Maybe she could quit drawing money from her savings account. Not that she needed huge amounts of money.

Jed tugged her closer, and she wiggled against his groin.

"Getting frisky, are we?" His lips nuzzled her neck.

"Well someone is happy to see me." She pressed her ass against his hardening cock.

"Behave." Jed stilled her hips with his hands.

"Why? Haven't you guys tortured me enough?" Her voice was soft and somewhat breathless.

"Honey, you haven't seen anything yet."

"Oh really?" She placed her hands on his chest and pushed. Not that it did much good. Damn, her panties were getting damp.

"Tell me, Kitty Kat." He marched backward, keeping her back plastered to his front. "Have you pleasured yourself?"

"No. Two men have forbidden me to orgasm alone."

He grinned. Closing the door, he maneuvered her into an empty stall. Jed guided her to one side. "Don't move." He had her facing the wall and patted her on the ass as he moved away.

* * * *

Jed watched her out of the corner of his eye as he stacked the hay up to the right level. Then he made a quick trip to the tack room, grabbing the materials he needed. He returned and placed a soft blanket over the hay to prevent her from getting scratched. Then he spread a towel on another hay bale, piling all the toys and restraints he would need for them to have fun.

The stall had rings in the walls to tie horses and hang buckets. And for tying up a sexy Kitty Kat. His heart raced at the thought.

Jed slipped his arms around her waist. She hadn't moved an inch. "Good, Kitty Kat," he whispered, turning her around in his arms and capturing her lips.

Lord, she tasted sweet. How long had it been since he tasted her? Not long. He'd kissed her just last night, but it seemed longer. His tongue thrust into her mouth, and she moaned.

"So delicious," he whispered against her lips before lifting his head and taking a step back. "Strip."

She blinked up at him and stared. "W…what?"

"Don't make me repeat myself. Remember our rules." He stared at her, and her eyes widened.

"Yes, Sir." Slowly, she pulled her T-shirt from her jeans, arms rising as she lifted it over her head to reveal a plain white bra. She toed off her shoes, unfastened her jeans, and slid them off her long legs. Plain white panties came to view.

He and Ry needed to do some shopping for Katie. He wanted her in silk and lace all the time. She folded her clothes and put them on the empty hay bale closest to her.

"All of it, sweetheart."

"Sir, what if someone comes in?" She shivered, and there was a slight tremor in her voice.

"No worries, Kitty Kat." He'd sent everyone home an hour ago. He wanted the place empty just in case. "No one will barge in on us. Now, finish up. You won't like it if I strip you down."

She swallowed, then bent down and removed her socks. Next came her bra and finally her panties.

His cock flexed against his jeans. Damn, she still took his breath away. Her nipples were already stiff, and her curvy body made his hands itch to trace every inch of her skin. Holding his hand up, he crooked his finger for her to come to him. She approached him with apprehension, and it was all he could do to hide a big grin.

"Give me your wrists." She complied, and he pulled the leather cuffs out of his back pocket. He buckled them around her wrists, making sure they were loose enough not to constrict blood flow, and led her over to the blanket-covered hay bales.

"Sit down."

She looked over her shoulder then back at him before sitting on the edge of the bales. He wanted to laugh, but he was the Dom here. His hands framed her waist, and she let out a squeal as he lifted her and sat her farther back on the bales.

"Lay back." Putting pressure on her shoulders, he lowered her until she was lying flat on the bales. Oh yes, this was perfect. He reached over and picked up the double snap hook, hooked one end into the restraint and then stretched her arm out to the side. He snapped the other end to the metal link attached to the rope and tied it off on the ring on the wall. Then he did the same thing with her other arm.

"What is it about you guys and restraints?"

Jed laughed down at her. "Snarky little sub, aren't you?"

Her face flushed. "Sorry, Sir."

"Better." He picked up the restraints for her legs, attached them, then pulled her legs to the side of the bale and locked them into place. Her eyes were wide when he finished.

"What shall I do first?"

She squirmed on the blanket, and Jed grinned. He stripped off his shirt and picked up the deer hide flogger.

He ran it over her breasts, skimming the tails along her stomach, down to her upper thighs. Katie let out a small sigh.

He lifted the flogger and brought it down softly on her right breast, followed by a light strike to her left breast. She hissed.

"Okay?" He wasn't the expert like Ry was, but he knew how to make it feel good.

"Yes, Sir. It tingles."

"Good. This is a deer skin flogger, made to tease and arouse your tender areas." He twirled the tails over her nipples, watching them harden. Then he moved down to her upper thighs and gave them a few good swats until she was squirming.

Her pussy glistened. He trailed his finger up her slit and then slipped his finger in his mouth. "Wet and sweet, just how I like it." He tossed the flogger aside and dropped to his knees between her thighs.

"Jed… Sir," she cried out when his mouth covered her pussy.

Sweet honey cream was all he could think of. He licked her from bottom to top, his fingers spreading her pussy lips apart. He loved her fresh scent. Using his tongue, he coaxed her clit out and began playing with it. Her pussy creamed more, and he slipped two fingers into her core.

"Sir, it's been too long."

He was sure it had been. He raised his head. "Come as much as you want, Kitty Kat, because I'm going to lick up all your cream until you can't stop coming. And I'm only going to stop when I'm satisfied." Which might just be all afternoon.

"Oh, fuck," she whispered.

* * * *

Katie stared at Jed's head between her thighs. She hadn't orgasmed for days, thanks to Jed and Ry. They had teased her mercilessly during that time but wouldn't let her come. She'd been on edge forever it seemed, and it was a miracle she hadn't exploded the second Jed's tongue touched her clit. But now that his fingers pumped in and out of her pussy and his tongue played with her clit, her climax rose.

She had to admit her pussy had grown moist the second he guided her into the stall. She hadn't expected to be restrained over bales of hay with him pleasuring her. She wanted to get lost in the pleasure Jed was giving her. Even though Jed had told her no one would bother them, she still worried someone would show up and see them.

Tingles ran from her pelvis up her spine and back again. She was getting close. She moaned as her climax washed over her. Her blood roared through her veins only to pool again at her clit.

Jed continued to fuck with his fingers and mouth. Her climax started building once again. Jed curved his finger in her pussy and pressed hard against her G-spot.

Her neck arched, and she let out a little cry. Her hips met his fingers with each plunge. She wanted more. No. Craved more. Heat flared over her skin, and her breath caught in her throat. So many feelings, she couldn't figure out where one climax ended and the next one started.

Her muscles clenched in a painful, yet delicious way that even curled her toes. She wasn't going to survive this. She began pulling at the restraints. Damn, he had her trussed up so well. She started to fall over the precipice and… She screamed as Jed sucked her clit into his mouth.

Her body was still shaking when he pulled his fingers

from her pussy and raised his head. He had a shit-eating grin on his face.

"Fuck, you're beautiful when you come," Jed said. Rising over her body, his mouth covered hers.

As his tongue tangled with hers, tangy spice hit her taste buds. So erotic to be kissing him after he pleasured her so well. His cock was hard against her stomach even through the denim.

When he lifted his lips from hers, she was breathless from more than just the kiss. She jerked at the restraints again. She wanted to touch him, to tease him, to take that big cock in her hands and milk it.

Holy crap, where had that come from? She never acted like this, but then again, there was something about Jed that brought out her wild side. He was making her yearn for things she never thought about. Even after going to the clubs, she never had thoughts of jacking a man off.

"Hmm, what shall I do now?" He rose to his feet, adjusted his cock, and looked over at another bale of hay.

"Please, Sir, take the restraints off." At least her brain was working enough to ask him the way she should. She didn't want him to punish her. No. She wanted to feel his skin beneath her palms, to dig her nails into his fine ass.

"Later." He grinned over his shoulder at her.

What was he up to? She was almost afraid of the answer. But her body hummed, and her pussy creamed even more. Damn, she was so turned on.

"Jed, you here?" A male voice called out.

She stiffened, and icy cold fear swept up her skin. She jerked at the restraints trying to get her hands loose. She needed to get free and hide. No one should see her like this.

"Hey, Mike, what's going on?" Jed called back as he stepped over to her. "Easy, Katie." He stroked her stomach.

"I just wanted to drop the trailer off. I parked it where you had it. Thanks for the loan."

"No problem."

Katie still struggled with the restraints. If Mike walked back here… She yanked harder.

"Everything okay?" Mike asked.

Was his voice closer? Oh, God. She held her breath.

"Yeah, I'm just working with a particularly stubborn filly, otherwise I'd tell you to come on back. I don't want you to get hurt."

Male laughter reached her ears. "Understand. Talk to you next week."

After what seemed like minutes, but was probably only seconds, Jed said, "It's okay, Katie."

Her pounding heart was all she could hear. She had to get free.

"Red," she cried out, still struggling. She needed to leave and now.

"Easy." Jed released the cuffs on her ankles then her wrists. When she was free, Katie tried to jump up.

Her knees buckled, and Jed grabbed her around the waist. "Easy, Katie." He swept the blanket off the hay and wrapped it around her shaking body.

When had she started shaking? Oh, God, she couldn't even think. Was Mike really gone? What if he was still there? She had to get out of here before she broke down. Now!

"Let me go. I need to leave." She pushed against his chest.

"Don't think so." Jed swept her into his arms, and she cried out. "It's okay, Katie." He sat down on the bale and cradled her in his lap.

"No." She fought his embrace. She needed to dress. It was all too much. She couldn't be in his arms.

"Kitty Kat," he tried again.

"Home. I need to get home, please." She glanced up at Jed.

His dark blue eyes filled with concern, but his jaw was locked.

"Please, Sir. I really, really need to go home." She fought not to wince at the sound of her own whiny voice, but she couldn't help it. She had to get out of here. He had to let her go.

"I'm driving you home."

Relief poured through her. "Fine," she whispered as his arms loosened. Katie jumped off his lap and ran for her clothes. She wobbled as she drew on her panties and jeans. The hell with the bra; her fingers were barely working. She threw her shirt on before grabbing her purse and shoes. "I'm ready."

Jed stared at her but stayed silent. He lifted her into his arms, carried her to his truck, and set her inside as if she were made of fine china. "Don't move." He walked around the truck to the driver's side.

His movements were a bit jerky. Katie regretted she'd made him that way. But she couldn't deal with him or anything at this moment. The drive to gran's house wasn't long, and the tension in the truck was thick because neither of them spoke. When they arrived, he strode around to her side and picked her up again.

Katie's grandmother was at her tea shop. Jed strode into the house and started for the stairs.

"Living room, please," she said. If he carried her to her bedroom, she'd really fall apart.

He glanced down at her, but turned and carried her

into the room and sat her on the sofa.

"Thank you," she whispered. *Go, go, go.*

Jed squatted down and cupped her chin. "You shouldn't be alone."

"Please, Jed," she whispered. "I need to be by myself." She had to sort this fear out.

His dark blue eyes filled with concern. "I don't like it." He dropped a quick, hard kiss on her lips. "We will talk about this." He stood and left.

Katie held her breath until she heard his truck fade into the distance. She curled up on the sofa, let out a sob, and then the tears started. She was helpless to stop them. Fear was overwhelming her even though she knew Jed would have protected her from being seen.

* * * *

Jed parked his truck outside the sheriff's office. Jerking the truck door open, he slammed it before marching into the building. He glanced at Betty the dispatch operator. "Ry in?"

"Yes."

With a nod, he made his way to Ry's office. Thank God he was here. Jed needed to talk to him.

Ry glanced up from the computer and frowned. "Shut the door."

Jed closed it with a quiet click and looked back at Ry. A piece of fabric flew from Ry's hands, and Jed automatically caught it.

"Put the T-shirt on."

Hell, he hadn't even realized he was still bare-chested. His concern had only been for Katie. He pulled the T-shirt over his head. Good thing he hadn't removed his jeans or boots.

"We've got a fucking issue." Jed plopped down onto

the hard wood chair and stared at Ry.

"About?" Ry sat back in his chair, but from the way he gripped the edges of the arm rests, he wasn't as relaxed as he'd like to be.

"Katie." Jed scrubbed his hands down his face. "I don't know what the fuck happened." All he could see was her frightened face, and it chilled him to the bone.

"How about you tell me?"

Jed explained how Katie had come out to help him with the bookwork and how it had led to a play session. "Everything was going just fine." He rubbed the back of his neck. "Until Mike came by, returning the trailer. After he left, Katie went crazy. Said her safe word."

"And you stopped the scene?"

"Fuck, yeah." Jed leaned forward. "I tried to give her aftercare, but she wouldn't let me."

"Jed."

"Ry, she looked at me with those beautiful eyes and begged me to take her home. I know it was the wrong thing, but it was what she wanted." It was all he could do when she looked at him like that and begged him. He'd walk on hot coals—hell, he'd cut off his right arm—if Katie asked him to.

Ry studied him.

Jed sat there, failure filling him. He failed Ry and Katie.

"You did the right thing, Jed, so stop beating yourself up about it." Ry leaned forward. "Katie asked you to take her home, and I'm sure you provided as much comfort as she'd let you."

He blew out a breath, knowing Ry was right, but it still didn't sit well with him. He wanted to be perfect for Katie. As one of her Dominants, it was his job to take care of her, and it hurt she wouldn't let him. "I want to know what the hell scared her."

"You said she'd just orgasmed, and you were thinking up what to do to her next." Ry's calm acceptance helped Jed settle down.

"Yeah, she'd come several times. I kissed her, allowing her to taste her sweetness. I stood there looking over the toys, trying to decide which to use next, or if I was just going to fuck her."

"Did she say anything?

"No. She stiffened and struggled a bit when she heard Mike's voice, but I walked over to her and calmed her."

Ry chuckled. "You sound like you're working with a horse."

"Yeah." Jed finished outlining what had happened.

Ry leaned his chin on his fingers. "Think, Jed, how did she feel? How did she look?"

"Panicked." His heart jumped as he remembered the look of pure fear in her face. "She was breathing shallow, and her body was stiff."

"Was it the same panic as with the blindfold?"

"No." With the blindfold, she'd calmed down the second one of them touched her and talked to her. "She didn't react to my voice or my touch."

"Had she been in subspace?"

"No, I would have noticed that. I'm sure of it." He went back over the scene in his head again and shook his head. "She was fully with me when I kissed her. It wasn't until after I turned away."

"And we've kissed her before, so it's safe to say that wasn't the issue."

"I know." Jed sprang out of the chair and started pacing Ry's office. "What did I do wrong?"

"Jed." Ry rose and strode over to him, placing his hand on his shoulder. "You did nothing wrong, so get that out of your head right now."

"But—"

"No." Ry's voice turned hard, and Jed snapped his head up. "This was not your fault."

Jed took a deep breath and let it out. Ry had gone into Master mode, and he knew better than to argue with him. "What do we do?"

"Since it's Friday, we pick her up and get her to talk."

"Sounds easy, but why do I think it isn't going to be?"

"Because Katie is a stubborn subbie. We have ways of making her talk." Ry grinned at him. "Besides, it's time to take the relationship to the next level. She needs to understand she can trust us to not only satisfy her but also to keep her safe, even from us."

* * * *

After a couple of hours of huddling on the couch, Katie dragged herself upstairs to take a shower. Once it was done, she curled up in her bed. She couldn't stop shaking.

She trusted Ry and Jed, but just the thought of someone else seeing her naked and restrained sent a shaft of fear straight to her heart. They promised to keep her safe, but they couldn't control everything. At the clubs, she never removed her clothing, so her fear had been muted. Was it being unclothed in front of strangers? But Mike wasn't a stranger. She'd known him in high school. They'd been science partners. Oh, hell, what was going on with her?

She closed her eyes and concentrated on her breathing. Deep breath in, then let it out. She continued her mantra until her muscles slowly started to relax.

"Katie, sweetheart."

"Gran?" Katie blinked, bringing her grandmother's concerned face into focus. There were shadows on the walls that weren't there before. She'd fallen asleep.

"Sorry to wake you, but Ry and Jed are here."

"What?" She sat up, clutching the covers to her chest as she glanced at the clock. It was seven? "I…" She swallowed. "I'm not feeling well, Gran. Can you let them know?"

Gran frowned. "Sure, sweetie. Do you want some soup or something to eat?"

Her stomach roiled. "No, Gran. I'm just going to go back to sleep. I'm sure I'll be fine by tomorrow." She lay back down as her grandmother left the room.

Several minutes later, she heard an engine roar in the driveway, and she listened to it fade away. She let out a breath and snuggled down into the covers. She'd been afraid Ry and Jed would come storming up to her room.

Part of her rejoiced they hadn't, but the other half wished they would have. Her bedroom door opened, and she jumped.

Gran stood in the doorway. "Ry said to let you know they expect you at their house at four tomorrow afternoon. And if you're still sick in the morning to call."

"Thanks, Gran." Katie closed her eyes. She had until tomorrow to figure out how to deal with this fear.

Chapter 11

Ry opened the front door at four the next afternoon. Katie stood on the porch, and his heart almost stopped. Her face was drawn, and her eyes were overly bright as if she were fighting back tears.

"Hey, Katie." He made his voice cheerful as he stood back and let her in.

He'd been afraid she wouldn't show up. But she had. Her smile was forced. Not good.

"Ry."

His stomach cramped with her one-word answer. His dominant side roared to life. Slipping his hand up her neck, he fisted her hair and tugged until he could stare into her eyes.

Her lashes started to lower.

"Look at me."

Her eyes opened wide.

"That's it, baby. Let it go. Let us take control." He could see it in her gaze, the fight in whether to submit or not.

A tremor racked her body, and he loosened his grip on her hair. "Can you do that, Katie? Today, while you're here with us, you'll give us complete control over you?"

"I…" Her tongue darted out and wet her lips. She started to nod.

"No, Katie." His fingers tightened in her hair. "I need words. I need to hear it from your lips."

"Yes, Sir."

"Yes, Sir, what?"

"Yes, Sir, please take total control over me. I need it."

His heart cracked. He loved her honesty about what she needed. It was another thing he loved about her. Loved? Yes, loved. The idea didn't scare Ry; it only made him more determined to show her how good the three of them were together.

Another tremor shook her frame. "You are so brave, sweetheart." He brushed a kiss over her lips. "I'm honored by your submission." Ry glanced across the room to Jed. "Are you okay with this?"

"After we talk about what happened yesterday," Jed said.

"Fuck," she muttered.

Ry tried not to grin at her whispered curse but failed. "Behave." He gave her a swat on her ass.

"Yes, Sir."

"Go down to the dungeon; we'll be along shortly." He released her.

She turned and made her way to the door, opened it, and disappeared.

"Shit," Jed said.

"Yeah." Ry rubbed his eyes. "Whatever is bothering her is not going to be easy to get out of her."

"I have to know, Ry."

"We both do, Jed. We can't have her running away when she's scared, without talking things through with us. We need to find out what caused her reaction yesterday so we can move forward."

* * * *

Katie sighed as she put on the sheer nightgown they had laid out on the bed for her. Hell, why even bother since she was practically naked. She shook her head. This is what they wanted. It was what she wanted. She'd wrestled with her inner demons all day yesterday and had come to several conclusions.

Despite her panic, she trusted Ry and Jed to protect her from prying eyes. Her fear of being seen by others while she was in a submissive role came from what she witnessed in her father's apartment. None of it wasn't safe, sane, or consensual.

Ry and Jed practiced SSC. Also, she was very aware she wanted to give control over to Ry and Jed, as it was part of who she was. It had never been that way with anyone else but them. Once she'd come to her decision, she had begun to relax.

Until she stepped up onto the porch. Her hands had shook, and her stomach had clenched. Then Ry opened the door and asked her to let them take control. All her fear practically melted away. They still wanted her. She hadn't even realized she was afraid they'd reject her until that moment.

She took her position and waited. She didn't want to talk about yesterday, but they weren't going to let her off the hook that easily. She'd slept all night, and this morning, when she woke, she knew she'd have to face them and explain what happened.

Heavy footsteps on the stairs caused her heart to flutter.

"Beautiful," Jed whispered.

"Fucking gorgeous," Ry said.

A rush of pleasure flowed over her at their words. Was that it? Did she want their approval? Yes, she did. Not many people had given her approval in her life, but these two gave it to her, and it warmed her heart. But she also wanted their love and understanding. Love? Oh, hell. Her breath caught in her throat. She did want their love, because they were the only ones outside of her Gran who mattered to her.

"Look at us, sweetheart," Ry commanded.

She raised her gaze. They were standing just to her right, both of them in sweatpants and nothing else. But they were tense, their arms held stiff at their sides and shoulders rigid.

"Come to us," Jed said.

Katie did, and when she got to the two men, her bones grew weak. It was all there for her to see in their eyes, their expressions, the way they held themselves. They wanted to keep her safe, even from them if necessary. Raising her arms, she wrapped one around Jed's neck and the other around Ry's neck. Then she pulled the two men into her embrace.

They placed their hands on her waist. She soaked up their warmth and their power, but most of all, their love and desire.

"What happened yesterday, Katie?" Jed asked.

"Do we have to talk about it?"

"Yes."

"Let's talk about this someplace comfortable." Ry scooped her up into his arms and carried her to the bed.

Within a minute, she was nestled between the two men. Warmth surrounded her, making her feel protected. This is what her life had been missing. Coming home had given her back the feelings of being safe and secure, feelings she'd been missing in New York City. Her heart jerked.

"Did I scare you yesterday?" Jed asked before Katie could fully follow her own train of thought.

"Oh, no, Jed." She turned her head and kissed his rigid jawline. "You didn't scare me." She'd hurt Jed, and that made her angry with herself. "I'm sorry I hurt you," she whispered.

"Oh, Kitty Kat." Jed squeezed her shoulders. "I wasn't hurt but worried about you and why you had such a fierce reaction."

"Why did you safeword, sweetheart?" Ry asked. "Jed told me everything, so help us understand."

"I don't even understand completely why I freaked out so much."

Ry brushed her hair away from her face. "Tell us what happened."

Katie outlined Jed taking her into the stall, tying her up, and how excited and scared she had been. How she'd been on edge for days and couldn't wait to see what Jed had in store for her. She squirmed between the two men. She was getting wet just from remembering the heated play session.

"I played with your body." Jed laid his palm on her right breast while Ry did the same to her left.

"Yes." Oh, Lord, her breasts swelled beneath their warm palms, making her blood sing.

"And you climaxed," Jed said, teasing her nipple to attention.

"Yes." She fought not to arch into their touch. It was so distracting, but damn, it felt so good. So right.

"Then I turned away to get a vibrator, and you screamed out your safe word."

"No…" She frowned. "Mike called your name." Fear slid up her spine. Panic and dread filled her veins, and she tried to fight it down. She was safe here. There was no reason to panic.

"What are you thinking right now?" Ry dropped his hand from her and cupped her chin.

"I did say my safe word." She watched the scene play in her head like a movie. "Jed had kissed me so I could taste myself."

"Did that repulse you?" Jed asked.

She shook her head. "It didn't bother me, but you turned away and…" Mike's voice filtered through her mind. Her stomach started churning; her breathing became rapid, and a wave of dizziness swept over her. "Oh, shit." She closed her eyes, fighting down the invading panic.

"Katie, talk to us," Ry demanded in a hard voice.

"You aren't going to like it," she whispered.

"Ry didn't ask you if we'd like it. Tell us. Now." Jed's voice was like steel cutting through the fog in her brain.

She registered the command. She took a breath and let it out slowly. They needed to know.

"At the time, I was afraid Mike would come back, see me spread out naked, you playing with me."

Jed's fingers grasped hers. "I promised you. No one would see you."

"You actually said no one would barge in. You never said anything about anyone strolling in or you letting them into the barn."

Jed let out a groan. "Katie, I would protect you. You have to know that."

"Yes…no…" Hadn't she'd come to that same conclusion? She went over the events in her mind once again. "Oh, hell."

"Explain, please?" Ry's voice grew quiet.

Katie lifted her gaze to meet his. "Fear. Deep, bone-chilling fear hit me." She reached up with her free hand and touched his firm cheek.

"Then what happened?" Jed asked, his hand rubbing soothing circles on her stomach as Ry stroked her collar bone. Their touch made it easier for her to concentrate on her thoughts and chased her fears away.

"I don't know. My mind kind of went blank. All I could think about was Mike walking back there, seeing me, and asking if he could play with us." She shivered, and two male arms tightened around her—one on her shoulders, the other on her waist.

"Never." Jed spit the word out. "We would never share you with anyone else."

"Jed's right. We would never hurt you like that."

"I know." She let her gaze drop. "Fear isn't always rational."

"No, it's not, Katie." Ry gripped her chin, tilting her head back until both men could gaze into her eyes.

"What made you call out 'red'?" Jed asked.

"I was so scared."

"We get that, sweetheart. But there has to be more."

Katie bit her lip. What else happened? Her mind has flashed back to her father and Walter and what they did to that woman. She assumed at first it was just Mike's voice. She thought it was coming closer, then wham, full blown panic. "I don't know. I just panicked." She wasn't ready to talk about this.

"Looks like we've hit another hidden trigger," Ry said.

"Trigger?"

"Let me explain," Jed said. "The blindfold reminded you of something when you were little. But you didn't remember it until we blindfolded you. We call that a hidden trigger."

"And you think that's what happened?" She looked at Ry.

"That's all I can think of." He brushed a kiss against

her temple.

"How do we avoid them?" She didn't want to panic on them again. Once was bad enough, but twice was too much.

"I'm not sure we can," Jed said.

Katie frowned. "I don't like you two getting angry with me." And she didn't.

"Kitty Kat." Jed's breath brushed her cheek. "I was never angry with you. I was upset with the situation and frustrated because you wouldn't let me help you. I wanted to comfort and hold you."

"And I denied you that." Oh damn. She was doing this all wrong. "I knew I was going to mess this up."

Both men froze at her words.

"Katie," Ry started.

"Honey, you didn't mess anything up," Jed said.

"But I panicked. I ran from you." She cupped Jed's cheek, relishing the warmth of his skin against hers.

"It happened." He shrugged his shoulders. "I'm over it."

"But," Ry said, "we need you to try not to panic and, instead, talk to us."

She nodded.

"And maybe it happened because it was the first time we'd played outside the house," Jed said.

"Or possibly you were overwhelmed and couldn't process what was happening," Ry said.

Katie shook her head. "I was excited for more until I heard Mike's voice, and then I panicked at the idea of him seeing me like that." She bit her lower lip.

"I'm sorry you felt that way," Jed said. "I had no idea Mike was going to be bringing the trailer back yesterday."

"I realize that, now. But…" She closed her eyes then

opened them. "If Mike hadn't shown up, I would have begged for more. It's hard for me to voice this, but I wanted more. I wanted to be bound and teased."

"Oh, Kitty Kat," Jed said. "There's no reason to be afraid to tell us what you want."

"Never be afraid," Ry said. "We want you to be comfortable with us and our relationship. Don't ever be scared to voice your desires and opinions to us."

Katie took a deep breath and let it out. "Okay. I'm sorry about yesterday."

Jed held up his hand. "Don't apologize." Jed started tracing his fingers over her stomach again.

"If something scares you, makes you want to run screaming, or whatever, tell us, Katie. We can work it out together, just like this." Ry's lips slid over her cheek before finding her lips. His kiss was soft, sweet, and gentle. Her blood heated.

When he lifted his head, Katie was boneless. Damn, she loved being with these two men. They made her feel like a woman, a desirable woman.

"So now what?" she asked.

"Just relax." Jed slipped his arm around her waist.

His touch sent awareness shooting through her veins.

"Tonight, we're just going to lay here." Ry shifted so she was half lying on his chest.

"I like this idea." And she did; it made her feel closer to them.

* * * *

Katie pulled her car into the garage behind Ry and Jed's house. She climbed out of her vehicle and sauntered up the walkway in the early evening sunshine.

In the last fourteen days, she'd had dinner with Ry and Jed every night, and many times lunch with one or the

132

other. In that time, she'd learned she could talk to them about everything and anything.

They'd gone out to several restaurants in Felton's Creek for dinner and even one day they had an afternoon break at Gran's tea shop.

It was these times Katie didn't take for granted. She learned a lot from the way Ry and Jed interacted with other people in town and how everyone treated them when they were out to dinner together. They were treated like family. Everyone talked to them, smiled, and there were even a few winks.

Not that there weren't bumps in the road. There had been some hard stares and even some who shook their heads at the three of them. But Katie chose to ignore them. What they did in their private life was just that—private. They didn't flaunt their lifestyle, and it was no one's business.

After unlocking the front door, she pushed it open, surprised to find both Ry and Jed waiting for her.

"Hey, guys." She strolled over to Ry, brushed a soft kiss against his lips before doing the same with Jed.

"Missed you today." Ry caressed her cheek.

"Me too." Jed took her hand. "And we have a surprise tonight."

"Oh?"

"Yep." Jed led her down to the dungeon with Ry following.

Her stomach quivered with excitement. They hadn't had any extended play sessions in the last two weeks since Ry had been stuck working weekends. Not that they hadn't played at all, but those sessions had been short. Now Ry had the weekend off, and it was Saturday evening. They had lots of time.

Jed pulled her to a stop by the bed, dropped her hand, and walked over to the closet.

"Strip, Katie," Ry commanded.

"Yes, Sir." Katie quickly removed her clothing. Goosebumps popped out over her skin in the coolness of the dungeon.

"I've got the outfit," Jed said, withdrawing a hanger from the closet.

"I'll get everything else." Ry strolled over to the cabinets filled with their toys.

Jed returned first with a halter-style, deep blue dress and matching shoes. "God, you're beautiful," Jed whispered before giving her a soft kiss.

"Gorgeous is more like it," Ry commented, taking her lips in a harder kiss. Katie's breathing increased when he lifted his head and handed Jed something.

Her gaze went to the item, but Jed fisted it so she couldn't see it. "Wha—" She shut her mouth when both of them gave her the stare. Oh yeah, she wasn't going to question them.

"We're going to go to a special restaurant outside of Monroe," Jed said, his fingers playing with her left nipple.

"And we are going to dress you," Ry said as he played with her right nipple.

She tilted her head to watch the two men caress her breasts. Only to find they each held a small, decorative, silver ring in their free hand. Well, not complete rings. There were small openings in the metal.

Ry slipped one over her aroused right nipple. Jed did the same with her left. Once the rings were on, they pinched her nipples, making them even larger.

"Nipple rings?" she asked. The intricate design lay against her skin, and the rings didn't pinch.

"Nipple shields," Ry said, glancing up at her. "We want you to wear them all night. Rings or clamps could cause an issue. But you should be good all night with these. If they start bothering you, let us know."

"I'm going to wear them all night?" Why did the thought excite her? Then she glanced over at the dress Jed had laid on the bed. Halter-style meant no bra. Her nipples would be showing through the fabric.

"All night, along with this," Jed said, holding up three pieces of string that looked like a thong. Some sort of jewelry sat in the middle.

Ry climbed onto the mattress and knelt almost in the middle. Jed set the string down, then guided her backward to sit on the bed in front of Ry.

Ry put his hands on her shoulders. "Lean back against me."

Katie started to recline against Ry. As she did, his hands slid down her arms to her waist. Jed knelt at her feet, then lifted her legs. Ry grasped underneath her thighs.

"Guys—" she started as her legs were pulled up and spread apart.

"Silence." Ry spoke against her ear.

Katie swallowed. Okay, they were in the dungeon, and she hadn't exactly followed protocol, but…

Jed picked up the triangle-shaped string, the jewel in the middle glittering in the light. She didn't have time to wonder as Jed began working it up her legs. He grinned up at her. "Ready?"

She shook her head no, but he just chuckled. Her head fell against Ry's shoulder as Jed's fingers parted her slit and wiggled the piece of jewelry over her clit. Then he held it in place as he maneuvered the string into place around her waist.

"Ry, lift her ass."

Ry slipped his hands underneath her ass and lifted. Katie kept her gaze up toward the ceiling. Her skin tingled from Jed's caresses around her ass and pussy.

Cold touched her clit, and she shivered. Jed adjusted the unusual shape on her clit, and she jumped in Ry's arms.

"Easy, sweetheart," Ry whispered. "Jed's just getting everything in place."

In place? What did that mean? Her clit began to throb as Jed maneuvered whatever it was they put on her. "Let her legs down slowly," Jed instructed.

Ry lowered her legs and straightened her up until her feet touched the floor.

"Stand up and spread your legs," Jed said.

Katie rose to her feet and did what Jed told her. Jed adjusted the strings, and one slipped between her butt cheeks. A string thong? But something surrounded her clit. Round and… She concentrated. Metal but yet there was something else. She couldn't figure it out.

"There we go. Perfect," Jed said, rising to his feet.

"Walk around the room, Katie," Ry instructed.

Katie took three steps and stopped. Holy crap. The thong didn't bother her, but whatever was against her clit tormented her. She took another step, and the jewel shifted, almost causing her to moan out in pleasure. She glanced over her shoulder at the two grinning men. Oh, these two were diabolical.

By the time she circled the room and made it back to them, her clit had swelled, and the throbbing was no longer confined to just her clit. It had expanded to her core. Her pussy clenched with need. Need for these two men to take her.

"Please," she pleaded. "What do I have on?"

"It's clit jewelry," Jed said.

"Attached to the thong." Ry strode over to the toy chest, opened a drawer, pulled out one similar to hers, and held it up. "The jewelry has a hole in the middle of it, and that is where your clit is. This"—he fingered the tiny gem hanging in the middle of the circle—"will rub and tease your clit with every move you make."

Katie let out a groan.

"Oh, yes." Jed scooped up the dress from where he laid it on the bed. "Arms up."

He slid the dress down over her head and then adjusted it so it fit at the waist. Then Ry took the halter and fastened it behind her neck. The fabric rubbed her nipples, making them harder.

Jed picked up the shoes.

"Umm, what about underwear and tights?"

"No underwear," Ry said, holding her by the waist.

"And you don't need tights." Jed lifted one foot and slipped the shoe on before doing the same with the other foot.

"Besides, we want our pussy available for whatever we want tonight."

"But aren't we going out to a restaurant, Sirs?" What did these two have planned?

"Yes." Jed put his finger under her chin and lifted it until her gaze met his. "It is a special place where we can play a bit and still be safe. Others might see our hands under your clothing, but no one will see you naked."

"Can you handle that, Katie?" Ry asked.

She hesitated. Part of her wanted to hide, the other part wanted to play with them. She chose the part that wanted to play. She wanted her men to be proud of her. "I believe so, Sir Ry."

"Safe words still apply." Jed brushed a kiss over her cheek before releasing her chin.

Ry slipped his hand behind her neck and held her. "I love your bravery and your trust. We intend to push your limits tonight."

Katie let out a moan, and both men laughed.

Chapter 12

An hour later, they pulled into the parking lot of the restaurant. The lot was almost full. Katie glanced up. The sign that said "Absinthe" on the outside of the brick building was her only clue it was a business. Ry took her right hand and Jed her left as they led her up to the door.

A man stood outside with a computer tablet. A bouncer outside the restaurant? "Good evening. Name, please."

"McKade," Ry said.

"Ah yes, Mr. McKade, party of three." He typed on the tablet. "Please go in and have a lovely evening."

Ry nodded, and Jed pushed open the heavy metal door. While the interior was in low light, Katie made out a hostess station.

"Welcome to Absinthe," a blonde woman wearing an almost sheer peach dress greeted them.

Katie's eyes widened. Where had the guys brought her? Ry's fingers squeezed hers.

"If you'll follow me." Her breasts swayed as she turned away from them and led them through the restaurant.

Round tables were scattered about, covered with white tablecloths. There were a few semi-round booths lining the wall. All were occupied by… Well, some men were well dressed as were some of the women. But there were also some in daring dresses, sheer like the hostess's.

The red and gold decor added to the sultry vision. It should be gaudy, but it wasn't. There was something sensual about all of it. A small group scened off to the side, and a few people danced. Okay, this was not just a restaurant but a club as well.

They arrived at the one empty booth, and the men released her hands. "Katie," Jed said, gesturing with his hand that she slide in first.

She sat on the soft leather seat and maneuvered herself around the table. Jed took a seat on her left and Ry on her right. Their thighs touched hers, and heat filled her veins.

The hostess set their menus down and departed.

"Do I dare ask what kind of place this is?" she inquired.

"Well, this is a very special place." Jed lifted her hand and kissed her knuckles.

"Very special," repeated Ry. His fingers tweaked her nipple.

"Ry," she protested quietly as to not call attention.

Ry grinned. "Everyone here is into BDSM in some way or form."

"There's no need to be embarrassed," Jed said.

"But what if we see someone we know?" This was getting a little daring for her. She never really worried about being seen at one of the clubs in New York. But then she only had a few friends in New York.

"No worries there," Jed said. "We pay for the privilege of discretion."

"No one here tonight will blink an eye at us," Ry said, his nails running over the curve of her breasts where the dress was cut in the front. "Nor anything we do here tonight."

"Do?" The word squeaked past her dry lips.

"Yes," Jed said, his hand slipping to her knee, and he inched up her dress. "Spread your legs."

"No actual sex, but we can fondle and play all we want." Ry's tongue rimmed her ear.

"Does being here and us touching you in public bother you?" Jed asked.

Katie started to shake her head, and then stopped. "I don't know." Then bit her lip when Jed's fingers brushed her pussy. Being found in Jed's barn tied up had scared her, but this… Something about this was different. Was it because she knew Mike? Or because she wasn't restrained?

"Look around, Katie." Ry said. "Take a few minutes to really study the people here."

Katie took a shaky breath then did as Ry said. Her gaze took in a couple sitting at a table a good distance away, and she realized all the tables had a generous range of privacy.

When they walked in, everyone had been dressed, but now… The man cupped the woman's chin and gave her a lingering kiss before his hand slid down her neck to her…breasts. The woman was bare on top, her breasts on display. She heard a soft moan when the man pinched the woman's nipple.

Warm hands touched her knees, and she jumped. "Keep watching the other couples," Ry said.

Katie nodded, as together, Ry and Jed slid the fabric of her dress up. At least she was covered by the table.

Her gaze slid away to another couple.

Two men on the dance floor and… Oh, my. One male was dressed in only a jock strap while the other male was in some sort of buckled harness, his cock on full display. The music stopped, and the two men, hand and hand, sauntered to their table.

"They're a beautiful couple," Ry whispered in her ear.

Her core tightened as Jed's fingers toyed with her slit. "You're wet." Jed's finger teased her channel.

She nodded. She was wet and wanting, and it wasn't just from what she saw. "Please." She closed her eyes, not sure if the plea was for him to stop or continue.

"Oh, we will please you," Ry said, his palm covering her left breast, plucking her nipple before moving to her right one.

"Most definitely." Jed toyed with the piece of jewelry, making it bounce against her clit.

Their touches disappeared, and Katie opened her eyes. Hell, when had she closed them?

"But will continue this later," Ry said, picking up the menus and handing her one.

Katie let out a sigh and, with a shaking hand, accepted the menu. How she was going to eat, she had no idea. Especially when she wanted nothing more than to have these two men torment her until she climaxed.

* * * *

Ry's fingers clenched against his thigh. Katie seemed a little unsure about the Absinthe Club, but she was trying. So far, she hadn't panicked. That told him a lot. He was pleased she was working with them on her fears and not letting those fears control her.

God, he wanted nothing more than to stay home and play with her, but he and Jed had talked earlier. Now that they'd gotten Katie to talk about why she ran out on Jed, they decided this was a great place to help her overcome her fear of them exposing her.

The last two weeks, they'd been out and about, spending some quality time with Katie, showing her she could trust them, and that there was more to their relationship than sex. Oh, the sex was important, but he wanted her to know that he was there for her and so was Jed. No matter what.

She could always come and talk to one, or both, of them about anything. He didn't want her worrying about anything. She belonged to them, and they would see to her every need and comfort. But it was more than that. Ry shifted in his seat.

Ry had no doubts about his love for Katie, and he wanted her to move into the house with them. Jed had argued with him about it. And as much as Ry wanted Katie with him, Jed had made him see he needed to give Katie time. She'd only been home a little over a month. She was still learning about her wants and needs. He had to let her test her wings a bit.

As far as Ry was concerned, Katie had gotten to test her wings when she went to New York City without telling them. Now that she was back, he wanted to do nothing more than lock her up in their house and never let her out.

Chill out. If he didn't calm down, he was going to blow this night out, and that was the last thing he wanted to do.

"Ry?" Jed asked.

"Sorry, did you say something?" He needed to get his head back in the game.

"Katie isn't sure what she wants to eat, so I told her we'd decide for her," Jed said.

"Of course."

Another step. He was more than happy to choose for her. Ry glanced up when the waiter arrived and ordered his meal. Jed did the same, and the waiter left the table with a smile.

"Why was he smiling, and why did you two only order two meals?" Katie asked, twisting the napkin in her fingers.

"He was smiling because he knows you're ours," Jed said.

"And we're going to feed you from our plates, so why order a third meal?" Ry said.

"Feed me?" Her eyes grew wide.

Ry cupped her chin, turning her face toward him. "Yes. Tonight we are going to feed you from our plates and hands, because you belong to us." He brushed a light kiss across her lips. "Your submission is a gift to both of us, so we will feed you in our own special way."

The music restarted, and people began filling the dance floor. "Let's dance." Ry slid out of the booth.

"Sounds good to me," Jed said, as he stood, and they both extended their hands to her.

With a small sigh, she maneuvered her way out of the booth, placing her hands in theirs. They pulled her to her feet. Jed released her hand as Ry led her to the dance floor with Jed bringing up the rear.

Then Ry twirled her into his arms. "Put your hands on my shoulders," he said.

When she did, Jed stepped up behind her and put his hands on her hips. Together, they started swaying to the music.

From the occasional shiver that coursed through her body, Ry guessed the nipple shields and clit teaser were doing their job. Catching Jed's gaze, Ry nodded, and Jed grinned at him.

"You fit so well in our arms," Ry said as Jed's palms inched down, and Ry slipped his hands up to her neck.

"Umm, Ry." She hesitated as he caressed her collar bone.

Ry held Katie a few inches away so their hands could

roam at will. He covered her breasts with his palms, and Katie stopped swaying to the music.

"Keep dancing," Ry said, capturing her gaze.

Her feet responded to his command, and she followed his lead.

"Do you like what I'm doing?"

She swallowed and then nodded.

"Voice, little one. We need to hear you," Ry said.

"Yes," she whispered.

"Good. Then you'll love this." Ry slid his hands up and undid the halter part of the dress, then captured her hands in his before she could grab the fabric. "No, little one." He guided her hands back to his shoulders. "Keep them there."

"But—"

He cupped her now naked breasts. Firm and perfect in his hands. A small tremor ran through her, but she wasn't pulling away, and she wasn't safewording out. A shaft of satisfaction hit Ry's veins

"Pretty," he whispered. "Dusky areolas and nice pink nipples, hard from the rings."

Ry plucked at her nipples, causing Katie's body to jerk with each tug.

"Fucking beautiful how your body reacts to our touch." Jed's hands swept down her sides, and he slowly began lifting her skirt.

"No, please," she whispered.

"Shhh." Ry brushed her lips with his. "Trust us." He danced them off into one corner. Ry faced the other dancers with Katie facing away from him, and Jed's back was to the room. "No one is paying attention to us. They're exploring their own desires."

Ry's gaze met Jed's, and Jed nodded. "I'm sliding my

finger over her thigh." Another shiver went through Katie. "Now, I'm…"

Her cry was small, and she rose up on her toes only to drop back down on her heels.

"In case you didn't realize, I pushed a single finger into her channel. She's drenched."

Ry's cock twitched. He wanted to be that finger, tunneling its way into her tight wet heat.

"Jed," she whispered.

"Oh, yes, baby. You want more." Jed looked at Ry and mouthed, "Two."

Ry nodded.

Jed slipped two fingers into her pussy, and her head fell back against Ry's shoulder, her mouth open.

"Talk to us, Kitty Kat. What's going on?"

She shook her head, and only small pants of air came out of her mouth.

"Oh yes, little one. Talk now." Ry pinched her nipple—hard. He needed to hear the words. To make sure she wasn't afraid.

Her spine stiffened then relaxed. "You two are going to kill me," she whispered.

"Killing you is the last thing on our minds," Jed said, amusement in his voice.

"Please." She kept swaying from side to side.

Ry shifted his stance. "Please what, little one? Caress you? We're doing that." His lips brushed her throat. "Or maybe make you come? Better yet, shall I fuck you?"

A moan escaped. "Oh, God."

Jed chuckled. "I don't think he has anything to do with this." Jed glanced at Ry. "I've got three fingers in her wet pussy."

"More," she whimpered in their arms. "I'm so close."

Ry nodded at Jed, and then he captured Katie's lips with his. Kissing her hard, his tongue thrust into her mouth, tasting her passion. While he controlled the kiss, his fingers plucked and pinched her nipples. With each pinch, she jerked a little in their arms.

"She's close," Jed whispered. "Her pussy is gripping my fingers like a vise."

Ry would have smiled if he could, but instead, he changed the angle of the kiss. Oh yes, Katie was very close. All it would take… He squeezed her nipple hard.

She screamed into his mouth, her eyes opened wide, and her body shuddered as she came.

"Yes, Kitty Kat," Jed crooned. "Come for us."

Katie twisted her head away from Ry's mouth, breathing heavy as her forehead rested against Jed's chest.

Ry eased his hands from her breasts to her back, rubbing slow circles as she trembled in the aftermath of her orgasm.

"You are so fucking beautiful when you submit to us," Ry commented.

"Your submission is such a wonderful gift to both of us." Jed lifted his glistening hand, and Ry licked his lips. If they were home…

"Damn, baby, I'm so fucking hard," Jed said.

Ry reached into his pocket, pulled out a handkerchief, and handed it to Jed.

"Thanks." Jed cleaned his fingers off then smoothed the skirt of the dress back into place and reached around for the halter. Katie groaned as Jed pulled the fabric over her breasts.

Their woman was so sensitive, so damn responsive, it was all Ry could do not to release his cock and thrust into her hot pussy. Once the halter was fastened, they stood together, swaying to the music but not moving from their spot.

* * * *

She was never going to survive. Katie tried to get her brain back in gear. These two men were lethal. Damn, her pussy still throbbed after her climax. They were in public, and she let them do this to her. She had to be honest with herself; she enjoyed every second of it. Hell, she was afraid to open her eyes and see everyone staring at them.

"Are we being watched?" she whispered between dry lips.

"If anyone saw you, then they were jealous, because you are so fucking beautiful when you come," Jed said.

Katie blushed and wanted to smack Jed, but she was still boneless in their arms.

"Katie, sweetheart, look at me."

She didn't want to, but she knew an order when she heard it. She tilted her head back and stared into Ry's handsome features.

"This is part of your training and submission. It's also to get you past the barrier of your fear in the barn." He brushed a kiss against her forehead.

"I'm sorry I teased you," Jed said. "Even if someone did see, it's not a big deal here. This is a place where we can express our desires."

She blew out a breath. Part of her knew they'd protect her, but another part was worried about exposure. Yet, this had been different than the day in the barn with Jed. Here, she'd been protected by both men. Held in their arms with their bodies shielding hers. And they had sort of discussed it beforehand. She did feel protected with them.

"Any regrets?" Jed asked.

"No." And she didn't have any. She understood now.

148

Her fears of discovery diminished. Ry and Jed would take care of her.

"You're safe with us, sweetheart." Ry's lips brushed her forehead before glancing up at Jed. "Our food has been delivered to the table."

Together, they swayed their way back across the dance floor to their table. Katie was grateful when she slid into the booth as her legs were still weak. Hell, her clit was swollen and still being teased by the dangler jewelry they had put on her.

Their heat surrounded her as they took their places. Their plates were filled with filet mignon, roasted potatoes, and mixed zucchinis. Ry picked up the fork and scooped up a bite of roasted potatoes.

"Open."

She obeyed, closing her eyes in bliss as the spices exploded on her tongue. Ry fed her the filet, potatoes, and vegetables while Jed caressed the nape of her neck.

All through dinner, one would feed her, and the other would touch her in some way. Never had she felt so alive or so cherished.

After they finished eating, Ry settled the bill, and they left. Katie couldn't wait until they got back to the house. She needed these two men.

* * * *

Jed grinned as they pulled into the garage. What a great night it had been. Katie working on her fears and submitting to them made him feel like a millionaire. Even now with her curled up next to him on the seat, his heart swelled with pride and joy. Ry turned the engine off. "She's still out." They hadn't even gotten a few miles before Katie had fallen asleep.

"Do you blame her?" Ry asked.

149

"No." Jed let out a yawn before opening his door. Once outside the SUV, he reached in and picked up Katie. She snuggled into his arms. Warmth spread through his veins. He enjoyed carrying her around.

"Upstairs or dungeon?" he asked Ry as they walked into the house.

"Dungeon. We need to get the toys off her, and I have a feeling she's going to need some attention after we do that."

Jed nodded and waited for Ry to open the door and turn the lights on. He made his way down to the dungeon and lay Katie carefully on the bed.

Together, they took her dress off and removed the clit jewelry. The nipples shields would have to wait until she woke. Ry pulled the sheet up over her to keep her warm.

"She's so fucking beautiful," Ry commented.

"Yes." Jed reached down and adjusted his cock. It hadn't softened one iota since they had taken her on the dance floor.

"She didn't panic on us," Ry said.

"Or safeword." Jed glanced down at her.

"And since she's asleep…" Ry stepped behind him. "Strip."

At Ry's words, a tingle started in Jed's feet and worked its way to his head. He quickly stripped out of his clothes while Ry stared at him with passion. Molten heat hit his blood stream. Oh, this was going to be fun.

"Where do you want me, Master?"

Ry rubbed his chin. "Bring the frame out."

Jed stared at Ry in surprise. He was going to tie him up and make him helpless. Would Katie think less of him because he was helpless before them? Jed glanced over at the bed for a brief moment before doing as requested. He maneuvered the big wooden frame into the middle of the room. While he did that, Ry lowered the chains to anchor the frame. They'd learned their lesson about securing it the first time the frame tipped over.

Ry used the step stool to attach the chains to the top of the frame and then tightened them.

"Go shower before we start."

Jed nodded and went into the bathroom. But he glanced back at the bed on the way. Katie was still asleep. He'd have to be quiet when Ry worked him over so as not to disturb her. He wasn't sure yet how he felt about her seeing him as a submissive.

Chapter 13

Katie rubbed her cheek against the cool fabric… Her eyes opened. The last thing she remembered was being in the SUV and snuggling up to Jed. She must have fallen asleep, and now she was in bed, in the dungeon.

Her gaze found a nude Ry at the toy cabinets. He was pulling toys out, toys she couldn't quite see. What was he up to? Where was Jed? Closing her eyes, she listened. Water was running; he must be in the bathroom.

Keeping her lashes lowered, she peeked at Ry, who was placing the toys on a small table next to a big wooden frame.

"Aww, fuck," Jed said.

Katie barely prevented herself from flinching at the sound of shock in his voice. What was on that table?

"Exactly." Ry smiled. "In the middle of the frame."

Katie's muscles froze. Was she finally going to see them together? Little tingles began working their way beneath her skin, but her stomach knotted. How would Jed feel, knowing she was watching?

Jed strode over and stood in the middle of the frame, the coolness of the room causing him to shiver.

Both men were naked and erect. Excitement had her pussy moistening. She'd wanted to see them together ever since they told her about them being together. She hoped Jed understood her need to see him submit to Ry. Jed stood in the middle of a wooden frame anchored to the floor and ceiling. She kept very quiet, not wanting to disturb the two men.

Ry buckled leather cuffs on Jed's wrists and then, using the chains, pulled his arms up and out. "Okay?" Ry asked.

"Yes, Sir," Jed said.

Her stomach tightened with anticipation. Is that how she sounded? Excited yet apprehensive?

Ry picked up a metal bar with two cuffs on either end. A spreader bar. He knelt and placed each of Jed's ankles in the cuffs. Now Jed couldn't move his legs whatsoever.

Oh my, this was going to get interesting. She pulled the sheet tighter to her chest and shifted to get a better view.

Ry had what looked like a black bag in his hand, and when Jed saw it, he let out a groan.

"Oh, yes, my little subbie," Ry said.

Her pussy clenched. That was the same tone of voice Ry used with her. Oh, how it sent a shaft of lust through her veins.

Ry dangled a black pouch in his fingers, then held up a cock ring, and when Jed saw it, he let out another groan. The cock ring had small bumps on it. Was that to tease Jed? She watched, intrigued as Ry slid the black cock ring over Jed's erection. Then he undid the black pouch and slipped Jed's balls into it.

"Did I forget to tell you? This is a new pouch. It vibrates to tease your balls. Your cock and balls will both be stimulated," Ry commented.

"Tease." Jed grinned.

"We'll see." Ry picked up a flogger and stepped behind Jed. Holy shit, she was going to see him flog Jed. Her core clenched; her nipples tightened, and moisture gathered between her thighs. She wasn't sure she was supposed to feel this turned on by watching them.

"I know you're awake, Katie," Ry said, staring at her.

Jed's head twisted, and his eyes grew wide. "Ry."

"Silence."

Jed stiffened in his bonds and shut his mouth.

"Come over here, Katie." Ry held his hand out.

Katie slid to the edge of the bed, pulling the sheet with her.

"No, sweetheart." Ry shook his head. "Leave the sheet."

Her lower lip slipped between her teeth, and she let the sheet fall as she rose. She padded over to where Ry stood, his hand out, and then placed her hand in his.

"Good girl." He brushed a kiss against her lips.

"Ry," Jed said again.

"I said silence." He flicked the flogger against Jed's ass. "Do you want me to gag you?"

"No, Sir."

"Sir Ry?" She hated the hesitation in her voice, but she didn't want Jed to feel uncomfortable with her being there.

"Yes, my sweet." Ry said.

"What are you doing to…ah…Sir Jed?"

Ry flashed a grin before looking at Jed. "Shall I tell her, or do you want to?"

"He's going to flog me," Jed said.

"And?" Ry flicked the flogger again, catching Jed on the back of his thighs.

"There's an Adonis pouch."

"What's an Adonis pouch, Sir?" she asked, curiosity getting the better of her.

"Well." Ry guided her around to the front of Jed in the frame. "Look at his cock and tell me what you see, little one."

"Ummm. There's a black cock ring on him, along with a pouch that is holding his balls."

"Yes. And there are two bullet vibrators." Ry took her hand and guided it to the two protrusions she'd seen earlier. "One to stimulate his cock, the other his balls."

"Like you do to me, Sir?"

"Yes. Just like that. But I take it a little further with Jed." He held up a brown-colored flogger.

Jed moaned. "You would use that, you bastard."

Ry's wrist flicked, and the flogger hit Jed on the upper thigh. Jed jerked in his bonds. "This is a double-sided flogger. One side is leather, the other suede. It will deliver a sharp sting or a thud, depending on how I use it."

Ry flicked his wrist again, catching Jed's other upper thigh. This time, Jed didn't jump.

"That was more of the suede than the leather." He shot her a grin. "Go grab a pillow and sit right there." He pointed to the floor.

She didn't move. She wanted to make sure Jed wouldn't be upset with her for watching. "Umm, Sir?"

"What is it, sweetheart?" Ry tilted his head staring at her.

"Is this… I mean is Sir Jed okay with me being here?"

"Oh, fuck." Her gaze snapped to Jed's face as he swore.

"Sweetheart, does he look disturbed?"

Katie forced herself to really study Jed's face. His features were strained; he was gritting his teeth, and there were beads of sweat on his chest, but his eyes… They were dark with desire and need.

"Jed, answer Katie's question."

Jed's jaw clenched, and his hands fisted in the cuffs,

but he stayed silent. Ry snapped the flogger on the outside of Jed's thigh.

"You will answer her, subbie," Ry commanded.

"Damn it." Jed's chest expanded then contracted. "If you can handle it, Kitty Kat, then yes, I want you here. I want you to see all of me. The Dominant and the submissive."

Katie took a shaky breath. Jed was allowing her to watch, to see him and Ry together, trusting her to understand. It humbled her. Katie glanced at Ry. "May I, Sir?" She waved her hand at Jed.

Ry nodded, and she walked over to Jed. Placing her hands on his chest, she went on her toes and kissed his ridged jaw line. "You've given me a great honor to see you, Sir Jed," she whispered.

Then she turned and trotted over to the bed, grabbed a pillow, put it on the floor, and sat down. Oh my. From this position, she had the perfect view of Jed's tight buttocks.

Ry strode behind Jed, his left hand caressing Jed's spine before running over his ass. He stepped back.

Jed's chest expanded as he took a deep breath, and after a few seconds, he let it out. Ry let the flogger swing, and Jed jerked in his bonds.

Katie was fascinated with how Ry managed the flogger, striking Jed's ass over and over again. It was like an intricate dance; his circular movements were fluid and beautiful. Every so often, Ry would stop and run his hand over Jed's skin.

"His ass is a pretty pink and hot as hell," Ry said. "How are you holding up?"

"Green, Sir."

"Good." Ry threw her a mischievous grin. "Maybe it's time for more." He strode over to the cabinet, put the flogger away and pulled out two new ones, along with a small box. He returned to stand behind Jed and set the box on the floor. The buttons on the box flashed briefly in the light. "Let's see if these can make you yell."

Ry hit him with both floggers, and Jed's body bowed. She really couldn't tell the difference between the floggers Ry held now and the one he put away. Well, he was using two at once, so maybe that was the difference.

"Fuck, Sir," Jed said.

"Oh, I intend to do that later."

Katie's head jerked at Ry's words. He was going to fuck Jed? Well, they had told her that, but she never expected to see it this soon. Her stomach tightened with anticipation. How would Jed feel, having Ry's thick cock in his ass, fucking him? She opened her mouth to ask when Jed let out a shout.

Katie shifted and leaned to the left. His cock looked bigger and harder than she'd ever seen it.

"Watch him, Katie. Watch the pleasure on his face. Watch him come." Ry touched the box controller with his foot.

"Son of a bitch," Jed yelled, jerking harder in the restraints.

"The bullets in the pouch are active now, and they're going to make him come even though he doesn't want to," Ry said.

Katie shifted on the pillow, her own desire rising. "Why doesn't he want to come?" That didn't make sense to her.

"Tell her, subbie. Tell her why you're fighting against your pleasure."

Jed turned his head toward her, and Katie sucked in a breath. His eyes were bright, but he was gritting his teeth.

Without thinking, she rose to her feet and went to him. His gaze never left her.

She brushed her fingers down his cheek before rising on her toes, kissing his clenched jaw. "Let it go, Jed," she whispered, her lips caressing his skin. "Let me see your pleasure."

"No, Katie," he whispered.

"Yes, my sweet Sir Jed." She ran her fingers over his chest. "I want to see all that pleasure. I want to see my Sir come."

"Oh, he's going to come," Ry said, dropping the floggers. "Step back, Katie."

She followed his orders. Ry grabbed a belt and slid it around Jed's waist. "Yellow," Jed said, and Ry jumped back.

Katie was surprised Jed was safewording.

"Jed?" Ry stood perfectly still after turning the bullets off.

"I don't know if I can do this with Katie watching." He looked conflicted and unsure. Katie didn't want that, but she did want to watch. Her core was on fire, her pussy wet, and her heart beating fast. Yet, if he didn't want her to watch, she'd leave.

"Oh, Jed," she whispered. "I don't think you realize how much this is turning me on."

His eyes widened, and she couldn't help but grin at him. "I never thought I'd see the two of you together like this." She needed to explain to him. "Together while playing with me, yes. But not in your own special session."

"Ry, is she really turned on?"

Ry strode around the frame and slipped his arm around her waist, his hand drifting down to her mound. Her legs parted automatically. He caressed her slit, and she let out a moan.

"Oh, yes, she's wet," Ry said, stroking her pussy softly before removing his fingers and holding them up to Jed. Jed's tongue darted out and licked the wetness from Ry's finger.

Katie let out another moan. God, these two men were sexy as hell.

"You taste good, Kitty Kat." Jed licked his lips.

This was still new to her, but she liked it. She loved seeing Jed restrained and Ry playing with him. She loved how hard these two men's cocks were, and she loved how excited she was. She dropped her gaze from Jed's, overwhelmed by her own emotions. "I'll leave if you wish me to, Ry."

She stopped breathing in the silence.

"Sir," Jed said, and she glanced at Ry. "I don't want to be the only one to come."

What? Her gaze jerked back to Jed's face, and she saw him smiling one of those killer "you're in for it now" types of smiles. Her stomach tightened.

"If you're going to stay and watch Ry make me come, then I want you to have your release as well," Jed said.

"I have just the thing. Don't move," Ry told her when he released her waist to stride across the room.

Katie started to turn her head to watch him.

"No, Kitty Kat," Jed said. "Your gaze stays on me, not on Ry."

Her heart stuttered then her gaze focused back in on him. "May I know how you're feeling, Sir Jed?"

"My ass is on fire from Ry's flogging."

His honesty surprised her. "Is it painful?" Ry never hurt her, but she wondered with Jed if it was different. He was bigger and stronger than she was.

"Pain then pleasure." He smiled. "I don't mind a bit of pain as long as there is pleasure with it."

"Are you holding up okay, Jed?" Ry asked, coming up behind Katie and making her jump.

"I'm good, Master."

"Then we'll continue, but first"—his chest slid down her back—"legs wide and I want you to do a half squat."

Her core quivered, but she did as Ry told her.

"That's it, sweetheart. And keep your gaze on Jed."

"Damn, I can see her wetness from here," Jed said.

Katie almost stood back up, but Ry put his hand on her hip. "Your pleasure is our pleasure. There is no reason to be embarrassed or anything else."

"I love seeing the pleasure in your face, Kitty Kat," Jed said. "Knowing that you're getting wet and excited while watching Ry work with me helps me let go and just be me."

She opened her mouth, and a squeal came out when Ry parted her pussy lips and slipped a hard, wide toy into her core.

"Just something to keep you worked up," he said as he pulled a belt between her legs and fastened it at her waist.

"Oh, fuck, that looks so damn hot on her," Jed said.

"What has Sir Ry done, Sir Jed?"

"Well, Kitty Kat, he's put a harness on you, one that is going to hold that vibrator in your hot pussy until he's ready to take it out."

Ry picked up her pillow and moved it slightly to the left. "Go and sit on the pillow, sweetheart," Ry said with a little swat to her ass.

She took one step, and her pussy clenched around the vibrator. The toy was hitting all the right spots, and it wasn't even turned on yet. She glanced at Ry over her shoulder. "I…" She closed her eyes then opened them. "You two are dangerous."

"To the pillow," ordered Ry.

Yeah, right. He didn't have a damn vibrator stuck up his groin, making it difficult to walk. Keeping her steps small, she finally made it back to the pillow and blew out a breath.

"Now take your position on the pillow."

Shit, he was going to make her kneel with that damn toy in her. Carefully, she lowered herself onto the pillow, groaning at the sweet pressure in her pussy.

"Very good, little one." Ry reached up and placed the small box into Jed's cuff-bound hand, positioned Jed's thumb on the control. "Jed is going to control that sweet little vibrator in your pussy."

"It's not a little vibrator." She shot him a hard stare.

"Keep your legs spread, because I want to see you, and I want Jed to see you while I fuck him." Ry picked up the condom package, ripped it open, and slipped it on.

Jed let out a groan, and Katie echoed it. Ry was going to take them both over the edge and make them climax.

"Okay, Jed?"

"We're green, Sir."

"Good. Keep your gaze on him, little one. I want you to watch his pleasure and his submission." With that, Ry picked up the remote for Jed's toy and turned it on before picking up a small bottle.

Jed jerked in his bonds as the bullets came back on.

Katie let out a small cry as the vibrator hummed in her pussy. Oh, God. The vibe was on its lowest setting, but it was already causing her core to tighten.

"You're primed already, aren't you, Kitty Kat?" Jed

turned his head and stared at her.

* * * *

She was so very aroused. Jed watched her body react to all the stimuli. Her nipples were hard pebbles, and there was a slight flush to her face.

At first, he wasn't sure about having Katie see him and Ry together, but after seeing how much this was turning Katie on, he knew it would be okay. Katie accepted his needs, his nature to be submissive to Ry but a Dominant to her.

Ry stroked his hot ass before pressing up against his back.

"Sir," he cried out as Ry caressed his hard cock.

"So hard." Ry slid his fingers up and down his shaft, making Jed grit his teeth. "Are you ready for me?"

"Yes," Jed whispered.

"Good, because my cock is hard and needy."

Jed jerked when Ry's lube-covered fingers parted his cheeks, but he relaxed as Ry worked them into his ass, lubing him up for what was to come.

Katie's eyes had grown wide again, and Jed bit back a smile. She'd probably never seen two men play before, and she was certainly getting an education today. And…

An idea popped into his head. "Ry," he whispered.

"Yeah."

"I know Katie is watching, but I want her to participate."

"What do you have in mind?"

"She can suck me while you fuck my ass."

Ry let out a chuckle. "While I think that is a good idea, I really want her to watch us the first time."

Jed moaned, but he was right. "Kitty Kat. Keep your eyes on what Sir Ry is doing, no matter what." His blood

162

heated, and anticipation made his cock grow harder.

"Yes, Sir Jed."

Ry's cock brushed his ass, and a shiver went up his spine. "Whenever you're ready, Sir Ry," he whispered.

Ry's fingers pulled his ass cheeks apart, and Jed took a deep breath and released it, forcing every muscle in his body to go boneless.

Ry rubbed the lube back and forth, breaching the entrance with just the head of his cock. Anticipation spread from his ass to his balls and cock. Ry pushed forward, the head slipping in and then out. Jed let out a groan.

"That was a good groan, subbie," Ry said, pushing back into his ass.

"Damn, you feel huge tonight."

"That's because Katie is here."

Jed's hips flexed when Ry's cock slipped past his sphincter. A slow burn radiated from his ass to the base of his cock. Ry shifted his hips, and a burst of pleasure followed the burn. "More," Jed whispered. "Fucking tight," Ry said, his harsh breath caressing Jed's back.

"That is so hot," Katie whispered.

Jed's eyes closed at Katie's words, only to pop back open when Ry pushed farther into his ass. The sensations of Ry's cock and Katie's heavy breathing were going to send him over the edge rather quickly.

"It's going to be a rough ride, Jed. I can't hold back anymore."

"Go for it."

Ry pulled back slightly then shoved forward, burying his cock in Jed's ass.

Jed dialed up the vibrator in her pussy, and a small cry left her lips.

Ry's hard dick reaming his ass sent his blood singing

through his veins.

"Fuck," he cried out, his hips jerking when Ry turned up the bullets. His balls tightened. He wasn't going to last long with all the stimulation.

"Do you like that?" Ry asked, pulling back and slamming into his ass again. "My cock in your ass and the bullets stimulating your balls and cock?"

Ry thrust harder and faster then turned the bullets up another notch. Jed's hands tightened, one into a fist, the other around the controller. Katie cried out, and Jed realized he'd turned up the vibrator in her pussy.

His ass tightened around Ry's cock. He loved the way Ry fucked him. Loved that Ry wasn't holding back today. Ry was taking Jed the way he wanted to be taken. And Katie? Her moans of pleasure were music to his ears.

Tingling started at the base of Jed's spine, working its way around to his balls, then Ry turned the bullets up.

"Fuck." Jed's hips jerked back and pure pleasure flowed through his veins. "I'm going to come."

"Katie." Ry's voice was husky. "I want you to go sit in front of Jed. Take the Adonis pouch off his cock and lean back on your hands, breasts thrusts out."

Jed was surprised at Ry's command. He watched as Katie did as Ry directed. Damn, if his dick didn't grow harder when she removed the pouch. Then she sat back, her knees automatically spreading as she leaned back on her hands, her tits on display. Her breathing was as rapid as his was.

"Fucking beautiful," Jed said, the visual of Katie spread out before him, waiting for his climax, ramped up his arousal.

"You both are. Now come, Jed." Ry began to fuck him with short, hard strokes as he turned the bullets on full.

"Ahh." Jed's neck arched. With a cry, his cock exploded in a powerful orgasm. His fingers fisted around the remote in his hand, and he touched the button.

Katie cried out.

Jed opened his eyes to see Katie writhing on the floor, her hips moving up and down. His seed covering her breasts and stomach. Then Ry delivered one last hard push, and the pulses of his orgasm caused Jed to orgasm a second time. Harsh breathing and the buzz of the toys filled the room.

Ry was the first to recover. He turned off the bullets and pulled out of Jed's ass. "Jed, ease up on the remote," Ry whispered in his ear.

His fingers uncurled from around the plastic box, and Ry took it from his palm and stopped it.

"Thank God," Katie said, collapsing.

Jed opened his eyes and saw her sprawled out on the floor.

"Well, I would say that was a successful session," Ry said, massaging Jed's shoulders before he uncuffed his arms. "Okay?"

"Yeah." Jed flexed his shoulders, relieving some of the stiffness as Ry undid the restraints on the spreader bar freeing his legs. Thank goodness his feet had been flat on the ground. "Check on Katie."

"Oh, I'm fine, thanks," she said. "Just leave me here in a boneless heap for a few minutes."

Both men chuckled.

"Oh, Kitty Kat, did we wear you out?" Jed flexed his ankles then stepped out of the frame.

"What part of boneless don't you understand, Sir."

Jed's grin got bigger.

"Go get in the shower. I'll bring Katie," Ry said.

Jed nodded. As much as he'd like to pick Katie up and carry her into the shower, he didn't think his legs would cooperate.

"Up you go, Katie," Ry said, squatting down and helping Katie to her feet. She wobbled but was able to stand until he rose. Then Ry picked her up into his arms. Jed turned and made his way into the bathroom.

* * * *

Ry watched Jed wobble his way into the bathroom before he glanced down at the woman in his arms. He was so proud of Jed and Katie. They were both perfect submissives.

Katie lay her head on Ry's shoulder, her arms loosely wrapping around his neck. Damn, she felt good in is arms, her body cuddling against his.

"Is Jed okay?"

"Yeah, no worse for the wear." Ry strode across the room and into the bathroom. Jed was already in the shower and the water on full and hot, judging by the steam filling the room.

"And what about you?" Katie asked.

"Me, what?" He glanced down at Katie, and her eyes were wide open, staring at him.

"Are you okay? Did you get what you needed?"

Ry froze in his tracks. She was worried he wasn't satisfied? His heart melted. "I got more than enough from Jed and from you."

Her fingers traced his cheek. "I know you climaxed, but…"

"Baby girl." His lips brushed hers. "Watching you writhing on the floor with the vibrator in you made me happy. Trust me."

"Okay." She sighed against his skin.

Inside the bathroom, Ry set her on her feet. "I need to take the harness off." He unbuckled the belt and pulled the toy from her. Katie cried out.

Ry dropped the vibe. "What is it? Did I hurt you?" His heart stopped.

She shook her head, but her eyes were unfocused. His arms closed around her waist as her knees buckled.

"Aftershock," she whispered.

Her body trembled in his embrace, and he held her close until it subsided, then tilted her head back so he could see into her eyes. They were clearing up, but he didn't like it.

"What happened?" Jed asked, pushing aside the shower curtain.

"Not sure. I only pulled the toy out."

"That's what you did, all right," Katie said then laughed. "And it caused me to climax again."

Ry grinned down at her, his muscles relaxing. "A wonderful side effect." He guided her over and they joined Jed in the walk-in shower.

"Umm. We're all going to shower together?" she asked.

"Obviously," Jed said as Ry set her on her feet.

"Yes, this way we make sure you're totally clean and taken care of." Ry picked up the washcloth and proceeded to show her just what he meant.

Ry made sure he cleaned her and Jed. It was his responsibility as the Dom. When the water grew cool, he pulled Katie out and wrapped her in a towel before handing one to Jed and then wrapping one around himself.

"Bed," Ry said.

Jed nodded. Ry started to picked Katie up.

"You've got to stop carrying me around," she

protested, holding her hands up.

"Why? I like it."

"Once in a while is fine, but you guys do it way too much."

Ry nodded but kept his arm around her waist as they walked out together to the bed. He slipped the towel off her body, motioned for her to lay down, and took his towel off.

Jed sauntered into the room sans towel to the opposite side of the bed. They climbed onto the mattress.

She turned toward him, and Ry hid a grin. She laid her hand over his stomach and her head on his shoulder. Jed slid up behind her, his legs tangling with hers as his arm slid over her waist.

"Sleep," Ry ordered.

"Yes, Sir."

"Yes, Sir."

Katie giggled.

Ry let out a deep breath. Satisfaction flowed through him. Life didn't get any better than this. He had the two people who mattered the most to him in his life and in his arms.

Chapter 14

On Monday morning, Katie sat down in the leather chair behind her desk and winced. Damn, Ry and Jed had given her a workout this weekend. A smile crept over her lips. Oh, but what a workout it was. From the club, to watching Ry and Jed together, to all three of them snuggling together and sleeping through the night. And Sunday… She couldn't remember having so much fun. They took the horses out for a ride and then had lunch in town. After, they'd been cajoled into a friendly game of touch football at the park. Game won, they'd gone back to the house and watched a movie.

Katie shook her head. She could daydream later. Right now, she had clients to contact and work to do. An hour later, she was knee-deep in computer files. One of her New York City clients had received a letter from the IRS, and he was panicking. Katie talked him down, and he scanned the IRS letter and sent it to her.

Now, she was gathering all the information. She wasn't surprised by the letter, but as she assured her client, it was routine and just a time suck.

She was printing the last of the paperwork when her cell rang. A sigh escaped her as she grabbed her phone. "It's fine, Larry. Would you relax?" This was his fourth call in the last hour.

"It's about time you answered my call."

She stiffened at the sound of her ex-boyfriend's voice. Damn it, why hadn't she checked who was calling before she picked it up? "I don't have time for you, Walter."

"Bull, Katherine. Grow up and come back."

His nasally voice grated on her nerves. "I am grown up, and I'm not coming back. I've made that more than clear to both you and my father."

"Don't make me come after you."

"Bring it on. You can't get your lazy ass away from my father." She hit the end button and rubbed her forehead. Walter was one headache she didn't need.

Her phone rang again, and she glanced at the screen. Great, now her father. With a sigh, she picked it up. "I'm not coming back."

"Katherine, I've already apologized. What else can I do?" Her father's grating voice attacked her last nerve.

"Nothing. I told you, Randall. I'm done." Again she hit the end button. Would they ever get the message? Eventually, she hoped.

Her father was only looking after himself and Walter... The man didn't have a trustworthy or honest bone in his body. Neither man had much integrity, and that was something Katie couldn't live without.

After double checking the paperwork, she emailed it to Larry and then called him. By the time she was finished, it was almost eleven. She stood and stretched.

"Oh good, you're off the phone," Gran said, standing in the office doorway.

"For the moment. What's up?" Her cell rang again. She glanced down at the screen and let out a sigh.

"You can answer that. I'll wait," Gran said.

"It's just my father again." Katie hit the reject call button on her phone. Time to block their calls. Probably past time to do that.

"Has he been calling you a lot?" Gran waved her hands at Katie's cell phone.

"Enough. He'll eventually get the message. I'm not going back."

"Have you told Ry or Jed about the calls?" Gran was frowning at her.

"No." And she wasn't planning to, at least not right now. She scooted out from her desk.

The frown grew deeper.

"It's okay, Gran." She walked over and kissed her weathered cheek.

Her grandmother stared at her for a moment. "I'm going outside and do some weeding."

"Okay. Don't stay out too long. It's pretty warm today." Was that all her Gran wanted to talk about? A little odd, but maybe Gran just wanted her to know where she'd gone.

Her grandmother just waved a hand at her as she walked away. Katie grinned. Maybe she'd fix something special for lunch.

"Katie," her grandmother called barely a minute later.

"Yeah, Gran."

"You better get out here."

Katie's eyes narrowed as she strode to the front door to see Gran standing in the yard by their cars. Her hands were on her hips, and Katie noticed the slight trembling of her hands.

"Gran, what is it?"

"Your car." Gran pointed.

Katie's heart sank.

* * * *

Ry hopped out of his SUV on Monday, slipping his sunglasses on in the mid-morning sun. He jogged into the Red Dog, the local bar.

Burt, one of the town's old-timers, sat in the corner,

nursing a beer, and he waved at Ry.

Linda, Roc's daytime waitress, wiped her hand on her apron and came rushing over.

"Where is he?" Ry asked.

"In back, the darn fool."

Ry silently agreed with her as he followed her to the back of the bar, down the hallway, past the small office and stockroom. Nothing looked out of place. Roc sat on the floor near the open back door with a bloody towel around his hand.

"Did you call the paramedics?" Ry asked Linda.

"Don't need them," Roc said.

Ry shook his head as knelt next to the older man. "Roc, how many times do I have to tell you not to confront these punks?"

Usually, Felton's Creek was pretty quiet, but lately, there'd been a rash of petty thefts and attempted break-ins. Nothing major until today. Roc's place had been a target before, and he refused to be intimidated.

"Hell, Ry, I cut myself on the knife I was holding. Those punks had nothing on me."

Relief poured through Ry. At least the punks were still unarmed. "How many were there?"

"Two. I'm sure they pissed their pants when they saw my knife." Roc gestured to the butcher knife lying on the floor.

"I bet." Ry unwrapped Roc's hand to look at the damage. The knife had slashed into his palm, a flesh wound, but it might need a couple of stitches. "Linda, get me the first aid kit." The waitress marched away. "Can you describe them to me?"

"Adult punks, I'd say in their twenties, both over six feet tall. They had on jeans, black caps, and handkerchiefs covering their mouths."

Different description than he'd heard from half a dozen other people. Interesting. Something wasn't adding up here. Linda arrived with the first aid kit. Ry made quick work of patching up Roc's hand. "Go see the doctor. I've done a patch job, but he needs to make sure you're good."

"Yeah, okay."

Ry helped Roc up off the floor, and the man swayed. "Never mind. I'll take you there myself."

Before Roc could protest, Ry had him bundled in his SUV. Linda promised to stay until Roc returned. After dropping Roc off at the doctor's office, Ry drove around town, checking everything out.

None of this made any sense. Were they local adults or kids that looked older? And if so, why now? School wouldn't be out for another month or so. Usually, trouble started by the end of summer when the kids got bored.

After pulling his SUV into his parking spot at the sheriff's office, Ry made his way inside the building. He waved to Betty, their receptionist/dispatcher, and went into his office, sat at his desk, and began filling out reports.

Josh, a deputy fresh out of the academy, poked his head around the doorframe. "How bad?"

"Flesh wound. Drove Roc over to Doc's. But I don't get it." Ry typed on his keyboard. He hated filling out reports. "Why now?"

"Did the guys get anything?"

"No. Roc flashed his knife, and they took off."

Josh sat down in the chair in front of Ry's desk. "Are we sure these are locals?"

"No." That was another problem. Could these be people from a neighboring town determined to create havoc or something else? "All we can do is keep doing our reports and watching for any trends. So far, no one has gotten seriously hurt."

"And that's a good thing," Josh commented before rising and leaving the office.

The phone rang. "Sheriff McKade."

"Hi, Sheriff."

Katie's sweet voice made Ry smile, and his cock hardened as he remembered their weekend together. "Hi, sweet Katie, what can I do for you?"

"Umm, well." She let out a loud breath. "I need you to drive by Gran's house."

His spine stiffened, and his gut tightened. "What's wrong?"

"Nothing super bad, but I promised Gran I'd call, so would you please come by? I really don't like talking about this over the phone."

"On my way." Ry slammed the receiver down and sprang out of his chair.

"What is it?" Josh asked.

"Not sure. Katie asked me to stop by. Something tells me it isn't good." Ry loped out of his office and into his SUV.

Within ten minutes, he was in front of Miss Mazie's house. Katie was sitting on the front porch. She stood when he got out.

"Are you okay?" he asked, his gaze sweeping her from head to toe. She wore a pair of jeans and a cute white blouse. She looked okay, and his breath eased in his chest.

"Yes." She wiped her hands down the front of her jeans. "You didn't have to rush over here. It wasn't an emergency, and I didn't mean to make you think I needed the sheriff."

Her words hit him in the gut, and he grinned. "I'm

glad you called, period." He strode up to her and drew her into his arms. "As long as you're okay."

"I'm fine. It's nothing, really."

He leaned back and stared down at her.

"Oh, all right." She put her hands on his shoulders and pushed. Ry released her. "Gran made me call. I didn't think I needed to, but…" She gestured to the driveway.

Ry's gaze followed the movement, and he swore softly. Her red, older model car had four flat tires, and someone had scratched the hell out of the paint job with a key or a knife. "When did you notice this?"

"I didn't." She folded her arms over her chest. "Gran saw it when she started weeding the garden."

Ry strolled over to her car. Damn it was a mess. Whoever did this had to have done it under the cover of darkness. "Miss Mazie's car?"

"Not a mark on it." Katie walked over to him. "She was parked behind me too."

"Damn kids." It had to be.

"Is that who you think it was? Kids?"

"We've been having some issues with some kids lately—petty thefts and such. Today, they tried to rob Roc."

"Is he okay?"

"Yeah." Ry made a mental note to call the man tonight. "When did you last look at your car?" He pulled the small notebook out of his back pocket and a pen from the front one. Even if Katie hadn't called him as the sheriff but as her lover, he was still the sheriff. He took his responsibility seriously.

"Last night, when I came home from your place."

"Nothing amiss then."

"Not that I saw. The security lights…" Katie looked

up and shook her head. "They were working, and now they're all broken."

The lights and fixtures were totally destroyed. Ry pulled his phone out and dialed. He was going to need help to get those lights fixed. "Jed, can you come over to Katie's? Thanks." He slipped his phone back into the belt holder, and then he put his arm around Katie's shoulders when he noticed her slight tremor. "Jed will be here in a few, and we'll get it all fixed."

"I don't understand it," Katie said.

"I don't, either." And he didn't. But something was going on, and he was going to get to the bottom of it. It might mean long hours for Josh and himself, but if it meant catching these punks in the act, he'd do it.

Jed's truck squealed to a stop at the curb. He got out and jogged up to the pair. "What happened?"

Ry gestured to the scratched-up car and the broken security lights.

Jed swore, and Katie's trembling increased. Ry frowned.

"I'm going back inside." Katie shrugged away from Ry's hold. Ry's frown increased as Katie went back to the house. She didn't even greet Jed. Why? He wanted to call her back, but Miss Mazie met her at the door and guided her inside.

"How is she?" Jed asked.

"Scared. She doesn't understand why someone would target her car, and frankly, neither do I."

"Who the hell would do this?"

"Don't know. We've had so many little things happening, but now things are escalating. What bothers me the most is why only Katie's car?"

"I heard about Roc." Jed ran his hand over the

scratches on Katie's car.

Ry nodded as his radio went off.

"Go," Jed said. "I'll take care of things here."

Ry hesitated. "Katie didn't call me here as the sheriff, but as one of her men."

"Well, that's progress." Jed grinned.

"Yes, progress I don't want to lose." His radio went off again.

"You are the sheriff, so go."

Ry grimaced. "Tell Katie I'll have a report for her insurance company."

He didn't want to leave, but duty called.

* * * *

Jed watched Ry drive away. The incident bothered him. Why would someone want to do this to Katie? He pulled his cell out of his pocket, called the local body shop, and asked them to send someone over with the tow truck.

He glanced at the broken lights. He'd need a couple of new fixtures. In fact, he wanted to put a few extras in. Jed started for the front door of the house. Ry had said Katie was scared, but that didn't explain why she went into the house without even saying hi to him.

Was she mad because Ry had called him? His muscles stiffened at the thought, and then the jealousy welled up in his gut. Did she want Ry's help more than his? Damn. Jed wiped his hand down his face.

His jaw clenched as he pushed aside his anger. First things first. He jumped into his truck and drove to the local hardware store to get what he needed.

Within an hour, Jed had the security lights fixed, had installed a couple more, and had the mechanic tow Katie's car to the shop.

"Katie?" he called, walking into the house.

"In the office."

Jed smiled when he saw her sitting behind the big oak desk, pencil tapping against her full lips as she stared at the computer screen.

"All fixed." He sauntered up to her desk, fighting the urge to snatch her out of her chair and drag her into his arms.

She didn't look up from the screen.

"Ry said he'd bring you the police report for your insurance company."

"Thanks." Her tone was dismissive.

Jed frowned. "What's bothering you?" he asked, leaning against her desk.

"Nothing."

"Liar."

Her head snapped up. "Jed, I'm not in the mood."

"Katie." He straightened from his position.

"Jed, honey, can you come help me for a minute?" Miss Mazie called out.

"I thought Miss Mazie was at the shop." Damn, this was all he needed. He wanted to talk to Katie and find out what was bugging her.

"No, she's been in the kitchen," Katie said.

"We'll talk about this later." And they would. He would get to the bottom of her sudden disinterest because it gnawed at his gut and heart. He dropped a soft kiss on her nose.

He found Miss Mazie standing in the living room. "What do you need, Miss Mazie?"

"Can you come into the kitchen for a minute?"

Jed nodded then followed Miss Mazie into the kitchen. She probably needed him to pull something off a shelf for her.

"Jed, I'm worried." Her hands tangled in her apron.

"I've fixed the lights." He hadn't expected this. "It was probably just kids."

"That's fine. But it's Katie I'm worried about." She moved to the sink, her back to him.

Jed stiffened. "Why?" What was going on that they didn't know about?

Miss Mazie turned from the sink, and Jed could see the concern in her eyes. "She's been getting phone calls."

"Hang-ups?"

"No, and I'm not going to elaborate. You need to ask her." Miss Mazie shook her head. "She's going to be angry enough that I told you about them."

"Don't you worry." Jed touched Miss Mazie's shoulder. "I'll talk with her. She won't be angry because you're concerned."

"Jed." Miss Mazie placed her hand on his arm. "Please tread carefully."

Jed smiled at her. "Miss Mazie, I would cut my right arm off before I hurt Katie."

"You're such a good man. Just like Ry." She patted his cheek and then went to check something in the oven.

Jed digested Miss Mazie's words before he marched out of the kitchen to Katie's office. Her head was down as she typed on the computer. He didn't want to disturb her working. But he wasn't going to leave without telling her goodbye.

"Katie."

She raised her head. Her green eyes somewhat unfocused and clouded.

Jed didn't like it. He made a spur-of-the-moment decision.

"Would you pack a bag and come stay with Ry and

me?” At least then they could keep her safe.

Katie shook her head. “I can’t leave Gran alone.”

He understood. “I don’t like it. What happened?”

“Jed.” Her eyes became brighter. “Please leave it for now. I have a ton of work to do, and I really want to get it done.”

“Fine.” He didn’t like it, but he did understand her request to get work done. “But you need to tell us if anything out of the ordinary happens.”

“Okay.” A ghost of a smile crossed her lips. “Thanks for fixing the lights and taking care of my car.”

“My pleasure.” Her mood seemed better, but something was off since her smile didn’t reach her eyes. Tonight, he and Ry would find out what was bugging her.

Chapter 15

Saturday morning, Katie smiled as she strolled from the front of Ry and Jed's house out to the barn. Her mood was much better than yesterday. The damage to her car and the security lights had shaken her more than she wanted to admit to Ry and Jed.

Even last night at dinner, she'd told them it was just the shock of the damage. But she wondered who would do such a thing and if it had something to do with her father. Last night, she'd awakened at every little sound at Gran's house.

Children's laughter floated in the air. A smile curved her lips. It was a new day. Ry had to work today, so Jed had invited her to join him and the kids.

She rounded the barn and found a lineup of kids standing outside the ring fence, jostling for position.

"Ah, good, my help has arrived," Jed said. "Kids, this is Miss Katie, and she's going to help me out today."

"Hi, Miss Katie," the kids chorused.

"Hi." Another smile crossed her lips. The kids ranged in age from what looked about six to twelve.

Jed sauntered over to her. "Your job is to keep them entertained while each one gets a ride."

"And how am I supposed to do that?" Was he nuts? There were ten kids there.

"You'll figure it out." He dropped a kiss on her nose and strode to the gate.

"Ready, boss." Katie looked up to see one of the ranch

hands leading one of the smaller and gentler horses out into the ring.

"Thanks, Finn." Jed placed his hand on the gate. "Maggie, you're first today."

The little girl squealed and danced over to Jed. The other kids all moaned, then looked at Katie.

She squared her shoulders and smiled. "Okay, kids, let's have some fun." She'd figure something out.

* * * *

After each kid had ridden, Jed leaned against the fence, watching Katie with the kids. Parents would be arriving anytime now to pick them up.

"She'll make a great mother," Ry said, coming up to him.

"Yeah." Jed grinned. She'd been playing hide and seek with the kids—with the occasional game of tag thrown in, well away from the riding ring.

"Is everything ready for tonight?" Ry asked.

"Yep. Katie came directly here, so she hasn't been in the house yet."

"Good." Ry rubbed his jaw. "I'm going to go up to the house to shower and change."

"Okay. We'll be there as soon as all the kids are gone."

Ry hesitated.

Jed stared at him. "What's up?"

Ry's gaze flickered to Katie and the kids, then back to him. Jed shivered with apprehension.

"Do you think any of the parents will think it's odd that Katie is here?"

Jed frowned. "I hadn't really thought about it." He usually made the kids stay right outside the ring and watch. But now Ry had planted the seed. "It shouldn't matter."

"I know it shouldn't. But I don't want Katie hurt by gossip."

"And you think I do?"

"Jed." Ry put a hand on his shoulder. "We told her we don't flaunt our alternative lifestyle to the town."

"We don't. We've been very careful." And they had been. Yes, they'd taken Katie out in public, and while out they kept public displays of affection to a minimum until they were alone or at the club outside of Monroe.

"Yes, but having her here with us and the kids? Some parents might be upset. You've never had a woman help before, and you know as well as I do this could cause gossip. It's happened before."

"Fuck." Jed gripped the fence hard. The last thing he wanted was for Katie to be hurt. "I want her here. I don't want to hide her away."

"I agree. We just need to be aware there may be a backlash." Just then a tan, mid-sized car pulled up. "Tommy Miller's parents."

Jed took a step and then stopped. The couple saw him and Ry, waved, and then made their way to where Katie played with the kids. They both watched as Katie greeted Tommy's parents. They talked for a few minutes, then the couple took Tommy's hand and went back to their car.

"See you next week," Tommy's dad yelled before they got into their car and drove away.

Ry let out a breath, and Jed sighed.

"Well, that seemed to go well," Ry said.

"Yep." Jed heard one of the girls giggle. Katie was squatting, talking to the girl, and his heart squeezed.

Ry's gaze was on Katie and the girl too. "I've found what I think will work in one of the catalogues I got last week."

"It's a big step." After Katie had watched the two of them play together, he and Ry had talked. They wanted to have Katie with them permanently.

"Yes, but we've wanted to make her ours for a long time."

"I love her," Jed said.

"I do too." Ry slipped his arm around Jed's shoulders. "And I know she has deep feelings for both of us, otherwise she would have told us off that first day in her grandmother's kitchen."

"What happens if she refuses?" Jed didn't want to think about that, but he needed to. His heart was too invested, and the last thing he wanted to do is have it shatter. Hell, he hadn't stopped loving her since she was before she was eighteen.

"We convince her. Simple as that." Ry squeezed his shoulders before releasing him. "I'm heading for the house. I'll be waiting for you two."

Jed watched Ry saunter away and grinned. How lucky was he? The two people he loved more than life itself were with him.

* * * *

Katie let out a sigh. Playing with the kids had tired her out, but it was all good.

"Momma's here," Lucy said. The little girl was the last one to be picked up. Ry had already gone to the house, and Jed was finishing up in the stables.

Janice Collins stepped out of her big black SUV. Her husband ran the local bank. Katie walked Lucy over to Janice.

"Hi, Janice." Katie put a smile on her face. While she and Janice had been in the same high school class, they'd never been friends. Janice preferred her cheerleader friends to a bookworm like Katie.

"Katie." Janice looked down her nose at her. "Lucy, get into the car, please."

Lucy threw her arms around Katie's legs before running to the SUV and climbing in.

"I'm surprised to see you here today," Janice said, picking an imaginary piece of lint off the front of her silk blouse.

"Why is that?" Katie tilted her head.

"You have heard the rumors about Jedidiah and Ryland?" Janice waved her hand. "Being seen with both of them in public and now in private can only hurt your reputation." Janice's sickly-sweet smile almost made Katie throw up.

"First off, Ry and Jed are two of the best men I know. They don't cheat, or drink to excess. We've had some nice lunches and dinners in town. Jed asked for help with the kids today." Katie kept her gaze fixed on Janice. "Besides, what I do in my private life is no one's business but mine."

"And what about your grandmother? What about her reputation?"

"Gran?" For a moment, Katie was thrown off balance, but then she saw the malicious gleam in Janice's eyes. "Gran can take care of herself. And this really isn't a conversation I care to have with you, especially when your child can hear us."

"Are you telling me how to raise my child?"

"No, I'm telling you it's inappropriate. And I don't really care what your opinion is."

Janice huffed out a breath and strutted over to her SUV. "This won't end well, Katie. Heed my words."

The driver's door slammed. Janice fired up the engine and took off like the hounds of hell were after her.

A male chuckle had Katie turning. Jed stood behind her with a grin plastered on his face. "I think you told her."

The tension seeped out of Katie's bones. "I so wanted to rip that woman's fake blonde hair out by the roots."

"I'm glad you didn't." Jed took her hand. "The kids liked having you around."

"I think they had fun today." She allowed Jed to lead her toward the house.

"Yes, they did." He squeezed her hand. "Usually, they have to stand around and wait, but today, they had you to keep them entertained."

"Jed." Katie stopped pulling him to a halt. "Janice is entitled to her opinion. But nothing anyone can say is going to make a difference." She placed her palm on his cheek. "You and Ry mean the world to me."

"That's nice to hear, because you mean the world to us too." Jed cupped her cheeks and kissed her softly before taking her hand once again, leading her into the house and then upstairs.

Her heart sped up. What was going on? Jed was taking her upstairs, not down to the dungeon. He paused at the closed door to their bedroom. She'd only been in their bedroom once—when she had gotten the tour of the house.

"Katie, tonight is for you."

Before she could say anything, he turned the knob and pushed the door open. The room was filled with candlelight, soft music, and the dark blue comforter had been turned down on the bed. Ry ambled across the room in all his naked glory, the candlelight making his skin look golden brown. His gaze, filled with desire, was on her.

Katie swallowed. What were they up to? She turned her head, but Ry captured her chin with his fingers. "All for you, Katie."

"Yes, Sir," she whispered.

"No Sir tonight. Just Ry and Jed."

Katie nodded. The herd of elephants in her stomach stampeded. She bit her lower lip. She hadn't expected this. Romance. Yes, she loved what they had done, but what did it mean? Jed had said he and Ry cared about her, but did it mean more? Late at night, alone in her bed, she thought about them having some sort of permanent relationship, but she tucked it away in the light of day.

Her heart pounded when Jed pressed up against her back. Was she ready for a declaration of love? She wasn't sure. But she knew she loved these two men with all her heart and soul.

"My Kitty Kat." Jed's breath brushed her ear as his arm encircled her waist.

"My beautiful Katie." Ry lowered his head and captured her lips.

Her mouth parted automatically under his. Her right arm snaked around his neck.

Ry's fingers plucked at the buttons of her blouse until it hung open, he lifted his head and rested his nose against hers. "You are so special."

"I think you both are too." Her voice was shaky.

Ry grinned, and Jed laughed. Ry took a step back and stripped her shirt off in a quick movement. Next came her bra, and in a flash, his fingers were at the fastening of her jeans.

Jed cupped her ass before he slid her jeans and panties down. He knelt and removed her shoes and socks and the rest of her clothing.

"Such nice, perky tits," Ry said as he ran the tips of his fingers around her areola.

"And such a fine ass." Jed squeezed her butt again.

The sensations of Ry's soft touch on her breast and Jed's slighter rougher skin on her ass sent her nerves into overload. With her body trapped between theirs, they maneuvered her across the room to the big bed that waited for them.

* * * *

Ry could barely keep himself under control. Tonight, he was going to show Katie just how much he loved her.

Ry kissed Katie softly. "In the middle of the bed," he instructed, watching as she climbed onto the mattress and placed herself as directed.

Damn, how did he and Jed get so lucky to have this woman come back into their lives? There's nothing he wouldn't do for her.

Together, he and Jed climbed onto the bed, one man on each side of Katie. Laying on their sides, they stared at her. She was so beautiful. She squirmed under their gazes. Her skin was already turning a pretty shade of arousal pink.

"Tonight is all about you," Ry whispered.

"It's always about me." She grinned, and both men laughed.

"True," Jed said. "But tonight is different."

"No dungeon, no Sirs, no toys. Just us," Ry said.

"Tonight, we're going to make love to you, Kitty Kat," Jed said.

Ry saw her breath catch, and he grinned before lowering his head to capture one nipple in his mouth while Jed captured the other one.

He and Jed had developed an unspoken connection since Katie had come back into their lives. They were so in sync with Katie, almost as if they could read each other's minds as they played with her body. Mouths and hands. Caressing her from head to toe. They wouldn't be able to do this with any other woman. She brought them together on a level that hadn't been possible with anyone else.

Katie moaned and squirmed on the bed beneath their hands. Ry's cock pulsed with the need to be inside her. He lifted his head, and Jed nodded. Katie was ready.

"No," Katie cried as Ry moved away.

"Shhh." He touched her lips gently before pulling her into a sitting position.

Jed stood on the mattress then lowered himself behind Katie before he pulled Katie against his chest, his legs spread out on either side of her hips. Unable to help himself, Ry took her mouth in a hard kiss before he trailed his lips down over her chin, neck, and between her breasts to her stomach.

"You are so damn beautiful," Ry whispered against her skin.

"Ry and I are always hard around you, sweet Kitty Kat," Jed said, his fingers plucking at her nipples. "My cock craves you."

"As does mine." Ry hooked his hands under her knees and raised them, pushed them apart, and his lips slid down to her slit. Now she was open to him.

"Ahhh." Her hips arched up as he licked her clit. The nub pulsed against his tongue. He licked her again, tasting her honey.

"I love how wet we make you." Ry slipped a finger into her pussy, enjoying the way she clenched around the digit. "Wet and wild."

"Ry," she whispered. "Jed."

"Right here." Jed his lips caressed her cheek.

Ry stuck his tongue into her pussy, wiggling it. He

retreated before he thrust it in again. More of her honey flowed, and Ry wanted more. He alternated between his tongue and finger caressing her pussy, enjoying the way her body vibrated from her cries of passion.

"Oh, God," she said.

Damn, she tasted so sweet. While he didn't want to hurry, Katie was more than ready. He wanted her to come around his cock. Ry sat up and adjusted her body up higher onto Jed's then looked at Jed.

Jed's eyes were glazed over with love for Katie. Yes, they both loved this woman, and there would be no letting her go now. Ry positioned himself between her thighs and pushed his cock into Katie's pussy. Her channel gripped his shaft.

All three groaned.

"Damn, baby, you're so tight," Ry said, pulling back then pushing forward again.

"Ry," she said breathlessly. "So big."

"You can take him, Kitty Kat." Jed cupped her chin, tilting her head toward him so he could capture her lips.

The sight of Jed kissing Katie heated Ry's blood. Sliding back until the head of his cock rested just inside her pussy, he thrust forward until he was buried in her. Pure liquid heat spread from his groin through his veins.

Jed's kiss captured her cry of pleasure, and Ry stilled, waiting for her pussy to adjust around him. God, she was tight and hot. His cock throbbed with need, and he fought his body's reaction to pound into her until she screamed with ecstasy.

"You're so warm and snug." Ry rested his forehead against hers when Jed released her mouth. "I have to move." If he didn't, he was going to explode right now. He kissed her before he slid almost out of her pussy.

Jed cupped her breasts.

"Yes, Jed," she whispered and then moaned as Ry slid home. "Oh damn, Ry, you fill me to the brim."

Ry's heart swelled at her words. Hell, his dick did too. "All for you, my sweet Katie."

"Look at these gorgeous babies," Jed said, running his thumbs over her nipples. "I love how you react to our touch, Kitty Kat."

"Only you two," she ground out between pants.

"Thank God for that," Ry said, pumping in and out of her. He wasn't going to last. Already, his balls were bursting. But he wouldn't go over without her. "Jed, make her come. Because I'm losing it."

Ry captured her lips but kept space between their bodies as Jed's hand slipped down her belly found her clit. Katie moaned into Ry's mouth.

"That's it, baby," Ry said, lifting his lips from hers. "Let us see your pleasure. Come for me. Come for Jed." He couldn't stop himself. Ry began pumping into her faster and harder, pushing her body against Jed's with every thrust. Every stroke had her pussy tightening more, squeezing his shaft. He was in heaven.

"Yes," she whispered. "I'm…" Her eyes went wide before her body stiffened, and she cried out.

"Aww, fuck, Katie." Her pussy clenched around him, and he closed his eyes in overwhelming passion. He sunk balls deep into her pussy and let go with his own climax.

Ry's lips found hers, kissing her hard and deep. His woman. His and Jed's. Nothing would separate them ever again.

* * * *

Jed watched the pleasure on Katie's and Ry's faces. This time, there was no jealousy over Katie, only happiness. Jed loved both of them more than his own life. His fingers stilled on Katie's clit, feeling the twitching of her pussy around Ry's cock. Jed heart pounded, and his skin tingled from the picture they made together.

His own cock pulsed. He couldn't wait until they took her together. But for now, he wanted to bury his dick in her pussy.

Jed looked at Ry, and Ry nodded.

"No," murmured Katie when Ry pulled out of her.

"Shhh." Ry kissed her nose.

Jed slid Katie off his chest. Ry pulled her forward so Jed could climb out from behind her. Then he held Katie while Ry took his place.

"Are you ready for round two?" Jed asked. He picked up the washcloth from the small basin Ry had put on the side table. With gentle fingers, he parted her slit and ran the washcloth over her skin, cleaning her up.

"That's feels so good."

"I hope so." Jed tossed the cloth back into the basin.

When he turned to Katie, her gaze caught his, and she smiled. "Come here, Jed." Her arms went around his neck.

"Do you realize how turned on I am, Kitty Kat?"

"I think I know." Her fingers traced his rock-hard shaft.

"Oh, Kitty Kat." Jed sucked air through his nose. "I want you so much."

"Then come here and take me," she whispered, lifting her groin to meet his.

"Not just yet." As much as he wanted to take her, he didn't want to hurt her. Jed lowered his mouth to her pussy.

Her fingers tangled in his hair at the first swipe of his tongue over her slit. Her honey cream tasted sweet on his lips. His dick throbbed with need.

"Oh, God, yes, Jed." Her hold tightened on his head as he laved her clit before thrusting his tongue into her pussy. Her muscles clenched, trying to pull his tongue inside.

"Please, Jed." Her voice was strained. "I want you in me. Please."

Her words were like music to his ears. Her hands fell from his head as he rose to his knees. "Your wish is my command." He wanted nothing more than to be buried in her moist heat, to feel her pulsing around him.

Ry slid his hands under her ass and lifted her. Jed fisted his cock, he ran the head over her slit, spreading her cream. When he was satisfied, and Katie was moaning, he thrust forward.

He threw back his head in pleasure. Pure ecstasy flowed through his veins. This was the woman he wanted to be with always.

Katie cried out at the invasion.

"Kitty Kat?" Had he been too rough?

"Damn, you two are lethal." She was panting. "Ry is thick, but Jed, you're long."

Ry laughed, and Jed smiled. "Just wait, baby." He began thrusting in and out of her wetness. "Wait until Ry's in your pussy, and I'm in your ass, and then we'll switch."

A shudder went through her body, and her pussy tightened around him. "Oh, God, I'm going to come again."

"Come for us, baby," Ry said, his lips at Katie's temple. "Show us your pleasure. Don't ever hold back."

"Never hold back," Jed said between clenched teeth, trying to hold off his own climax. He pumped harder and faster. "Come for me, Katie."

"I..."

Jed captured her cry of pleasure with his lips as his own ripped through him.

* * * *

Katie couldn't breathe after Jed released her mouth. Love for these two men flowed through her veins. And the sex was great too. Her lips twitched.

It was so much more. She wasn't sure how to explain it even to herself. All she knew was she felt safe and protected with them.

Oh, God, how she loved these two men. The words filtered through her brain. She wasn't surprised by the thought. Not anymore. These two men would always take care of her. Her love would only make that caring so much sweeter.

Katie drew in some needed oxygen. This was the new beginning she wanted with Ry and Jed. Two pairs of arms encircled her body, and without breaking contact, they rolled onto their sides. Jed faced her with his cock inside her throbbing pussy. Ry was behind her, his arms around her, and his fingers playing with her breasts.

"Rest, Kitty Kat," Jed whispered.

His cock slipped from her, and she sighed. Maybe after a little nap, they could do this again. But this time, she would lead and show them her love.

Chapter 16

Katie blew out a breath. Two and a half weeks had passed since the vandalism with her car. Everything seemed to have calmed down. But everyone in town was on alert, and so far there had been no more incidents.

She shifted in her chair. She'd set her spam blocker to block the voice calls, and she no longer received notifications of their texts. Even so, they could still text her and she wouldn't see it until she looked in her spam folder.

Now, she was getting hang-up calls from a number she didn't recognize. At first, she just thought it was a wrong number, but it happened several times a day. When she researched the number all it said was spam. She had thought about changing her number but didn't want to go through the hassle.

Enough of those depressing thoughts. Katie grinned. It was Friday night, and she was able to spend time with Ry and Jed. She shifted again. In the last two weeks, the two had decided it was time to work on her ass.

They had started slowly at first, using their fingers and anal beads, then worked their way up to butt plugs. Right now, a glass butt plug rested in her ass and drove her crazy. At least it would come out tonight.

After Gran had left for her tea shop, Jed had stopped by this morning to insert the largest one for her. When she stared at the glass plug, he explained it would be more comfortable than plastic, and if she experienced any pain or cramping to remove it and let him know.

Then he informed her Ry had the weekend off and to tell Gran not to expect her home.

Even with everything going on, the more time she spent with them, the more she realized how much she loved these two men. Two men. Part of her wondered if she was crazy, but the other part knew she'd loved them since she was a teen.

Losing eight years with them still made her sad, but it was something she'd had to do. And she still hadn't told them the whole story, mainly because her father was such an asshole and liar, and she had fallen for it. Maybe another time. Not this weekend. This time was for them. She would be completely theirs this weekend as they took her together. She didn't want to distract them or herself with talk of her father.

Glancing at the clock told her it was three. Good. She could close up for the day, as most of her clients were already gone for the weekend, and those few who were around could wait until Monday. She shut down her computer and left her office. She wanted to be ready for tonight, so she was going to shower and shave at her house.

She doubled checked the front door before going upstairs to her bathroom. It was a shame this crime spree, or whatever it was, was happening. It had shaken the residents of Felton's Creek, but they were a resilient bunch.

The annual June celebration held in honor of Felton's Creek's founder was still going ahead full speed, and she couldn't wait. It had been a long time since she could attend. The booths and attractions were fun for kids and adults alike. Jed would be there with ponies for the kids to ride. She would be helping Gran at her stand, and Ry would be there with the sheriff's SUV for everyone to look at.

Katie sighed as she stepped under the hot spray. The water beating down on her shoulders helped relieve some of the tension from sitting at her desk all day. But she had to smile. Business was good. She'd picked up several new clients, so she had no complaints.

She raised her leg to shave it, and the butt plug shifted again. Arousal shot from her ass to her clit to her breasts. Her fingers strayed to her pussy lips.

Wetness, not just from the water, greeted her. Shifting her stance, she braced one hand against the shower wall and began stroking her fingers along her folds before plunging one into her pussy. She closed her eyes and let her head fall back.

* * * *

Ry stood in the doorway of the bathroom, watching Katie through the clear shower doors. He'd stopped by to talk with her about tonight. The front door was locked, and Katie's car was in the driveway, so he'd used the key Miss Mazie had given him and had let himself in. Once he'd seen the little vixen masturbating in the shower, his cock had gone hard within a second.

She had her hand buried between her legs, her harsh breathing filling the air along with steam. Her mouth was parted and her skin flushed. A groan of pleasure left her lips.

He was sure they had told her no pleasuring herself. His little one was going to be punished for this. Of course, she probably hadn't thought about that. He hadn't told her he was going to stop by.

A grin formed over his lips. Oh, tonight was going to be fun—along with the rest of the weekend. Ry rested his shoulder against the door frame and watched Katie as she stroked herself.

Her head was thrown back, and she moaned. "Yes, Ry, that's it. Stroke me. Harder. Faster."

Her hips began to move in time with her hand. "Oh, Jed, you feel so good in my ass."

Ry almost swallowed his tongue. Jed had called him to let him know he'd put the largest plug in Katie's ass this morning, so they could both take her this weekend. And here she was, fantasizing about them.

He kept his gaze on her as she kept talking and stroking herself. Her body went rigid, and she cried out, "Yes! I'm coming." Her head fell forward, her hand braced against the shower tile. After a minute or two, she straightened.

Ry toyed with joining her, but decided no, he would wait. Anticipation would make the night all the sweeter. He silently backed away. Wait until he told Jed about this. They would decide together how to punish their naughty submissive.

* * * *

Jed pushed open the door to Miss Mazie's tea shop. Miss Mazie had called him a little while ago and asked him to stop by. The small shop had tables scattered around with chairs that looked too dainty to hold his weight. A counter and display case were near the back wall.

"Thanks for coming by, Jed," Miss Mazie said, walking toward him.

"Not a problem, Miss Mazie. What can I do for you?"

"Let's sit down." She waved in the direction of an empty table just big enough for two. Jed held her chair for her before taking his own. Miss Maize looked worried.

"Is something bothering you?" He reached across the

table and patted the back of her wrinkled hand.

"You're such a dear boy, and so is Ry." Her smile was sad.

It took everything Jed had not to stiffen and demand to know what she meant. Hell, were there rumors going around about the three of them? It wouldn't be the first time he and Ry were the topic of the gossip mill, but he didn't want Katie involved.

"I'm thinking my Katie didn't tell you about what is happening?" Miss Mazie asked.

Jed froze. What the hell hadn't Katie told them? "What is it?" He fought to keep his tone even and not demand that Miss Mazie tell him everything.

"Well, after the incident at the house, she's been getting hang-up calls on her cell."

"You mentioned calls to me before, but you said they weren't hang-ups."

Miss Mazie nodded. "The others Katie needs to tell you about, but the hang-up calls I'm not betraying any trust by telling you."

"The hang-ups have been happening since the vandalism incident?" Jed rubbed his chin, relaxing slightly. Ry hadn't mentioned anything, which meant Katie was keeping information from them. That was not good.

"I noticed it a few days after the car and broken light. I know they're still continuing."

"Have you told Ry about this?"

Miss Mazie shook her head. "I called him and left him a message then called you."

"Thank you, Miss Mazie. We'll both talk to Katie about the calls." Jed didn't like this at all.

"I knew I could count on you boys to take care of my

girl." Miss Mazie stood up, and Jed automatically rose. "Have fun this weekend." With that, she moseyed back to the counter.

Jed shook his head. Miss Mazie never failed to amaze him. Most grandmothers would be livid at their granddaughter for being with two men, but not Miss Mazie. She was always accepting of them.

He made his way out of the tea shop to his truck. Once there, he pulled out his cell and called Ry. "Hey, you on your way home?"

"Yeah," Ry answered. "We need to talk before Katie comes over tonight."

"Yes, we do. Be there in ten."

* * * *

Katie glanced at the clock as she hurried into her bedroom to dress. Four-fifteen. Her shower had taken her longer than she expected because of the damn butt plug. Every time she moved, it aroused her more.

Masturbating had taken the edge off, but not by much. She was going to be more than aroused when she got to Ry and Jed's house tonight.

She dressed quickly in the clothes Jed asked her to wear for the evening. Nothing special, just a skirt and T-shirt. But no bra and no panties. She stopped in the kitchen to check the meal in the slow cooker and left Gran a note, telling her when dinner would be ready. She'd already told Gran she wouldn't be home tonight.

At the front door of her house, Katie paused. She'd planned on walking to Ry and Jed's house, but that would be torture with the butt plug and no underwear. She preferred to walk, even though she parked her car behind the house, people were nosy. It wasn't like they were hiding their relationship, but as Ry had said in the beginning, they didn't flaunt their lifestyle, either.

She walked down the porch stairs, and a sensual quiver sparked out from her pussy to her clit to her nipples. Her breath hiccupped. Oh damn. She was already on edge, and she couldn't wait until they allowed her to climax. With slow measured steps, she made it to her car.

Her lips tilted up. Their brand of dominance made her feel special, and she enjoyed it. It was different than anything she'd ever experienced. Even in the clubs she'd gone to, she'd watched Dominants and submissives play, and rarely had she seen the affection she had with Ry and Jed. It was that elusive power exchange she'd heard about but never really saw. Her pleasure was their pleasure. Her pain was their pain. And the aftercare… They took care of her after every scene, be it a short or long one.

She loved cuddling with them, and they talked about anything and everything. Hell, last weekend, they had her telling them her favorite fantasies. Her stomach fluttered. She'd never been so open and honest with the few men in her life. Now she had two of them.

It excited her that they could have a relationship like that. Not at all like the relationship with Walter. Walter hadn't really been interested in her, just what her father could give him. Fame, money, and connections—that's what Walter wanted.

And then there was her old need to win her dysfunctional father's love. It had taken her years to realize her father would never love her like he loved himself. She sighed. Between the hang-up calls and the texts from her ex and father, her nerves were getting worn down.

Katie pushed all those negative thoughts away. She was looking forward to a relaxing weekend with her men.

After parking her car, she strode up the walkway to

the house. It was time to put everything but Ry and Jed out of her mind. She opened the door then locked it behind her. After dropping her purse on the small table, she went to the dungeon door, punched in the code, and opened the door.

She frowned. The lights were already on. Oh, they must have forgotten to turn them off. She made her way down the stairs, wondering what Ry and Jed had planned for her. Her feet sank onto the soft padded floor, and she went still.

Ry and Jed were standing by the bed, arms crossed over their chests and feet apart in their "We are your Doms" pose. Oh, shit. What had she done to set them off?

"Hi, guys," she said, trying to inject a note of cheerfulness into her voice.

They both stared at her, their glares hard and unyielding. A sliver of apprehension slithered through her veins. Oh, this was so not good.

She opened her mouth.

"Silence."

Katie stiffened at Ry's sharp tone.

"No excuses, Kitty Kat," Jed said, his voice much less harsh. "Tonight, you will only voice your pleasure and answer our questions."

Ry strode over to her, and it took everything Katie had in her to hold her place. He cupped her chin and raised her face to his. "Safe words?"

She swallowed. "Red and yellow."

"Good girl." He brushed a kiss across her lips before he started undressing her. When he finished stripping her, Jed approached with a blindfold. Damn, she hated the loss of her sight. She fought down her anxiety. Ry and Jed would take care of her. Once it was on, they lifted her and carried her across the room.

Katie battled with her instincts to struggle. Then they shifted her in their embrace and set her down on her knees. A loud click sounded in the room and coolness encased her ankles. Before she could take a breath, they were pushing her down until her elbows rested on padded mats and her wrists were enclosed into metal as well.

Her ass was raised in the air, and she shivered with the thought of what she looked like, ankles and wrists restrained and her ass sticking up, begging for attention.

"We haven't restrained your neck, so don't make us," Jed said, and the blindfold was removed.

She sighed in relief at the return of her sight. She turned her head and realized she was in a kneeling stockade of sorts. Her legs were spread, as were her arms. Her breath hiccupped in her throat.

"Do you know why we've put you in the stockade, subbie?" Ry asked.

She shook her head.

"Answer." Ry smacked her on the ass, causing the plug in her ass to wiggle. She gasped at the pressure.

"No, Sir."

"Kitty Kat has been naughty," Jed said, running his fingers up her spine, causing a shiver of unease to flow through her.

"Sir?" What was Jed talking about?

"You pleasured yourself today, Kitty Kat, without our permission."

Katie opened her mouth and then shut it. How the hell did they find that out? And then she berated herself for being so stupid. She knew better. She let her head drop. "Yes, Sir, I did. I'm sorry."

"That's the reason I'm punishing you, subbie. Do you

know why Jed is going to punish you?" Ry asked.

Oh crap, what else could she have done? "No, Sir, I don't know why you're going to punish your disobedient sub."

"Is there something you want to tell us?" Jed asked.

Katie wracked her brains, trying to figure out what she hadn't shared with them. Okay, there were some things with her father and her ex, but those things really didn't matter. "I'm sorry, Sir, I can't think of anything."

Ry's growl of displeasure reached her ears, and another shiver wracked her body.

"I'm glad to see you've still got the butt plug in," Jed said, his hand caressing her ass cheeks.

"Yes, Sir."

Ry smacked her ass. Fire raced over her skin. Ry hit a lot harder than Jed. "Did our little subbie forget to tell us about some hang-up calls?"

Katie rolled her eyes. That's what this was about? "I didn't think they were important." And she didn't. They were annoying, was all.

"Everything is important." Ry smacked her ass again.

"He's right, Kitty Kat." Jed's voice was close to her ear. She raised her head, and he was kneeling next to her. "You must tell us everything. Otherwise, how will we protect you?"

"But I don't need protection."

Ry smacked her ass, and she let out a yelp. Damn, that stung, but the blow also sent hot pulses of anticipation through her veins. "You are ours. We protect what is ours, no matter what."

"Ours, Kitty Kat," Jed said. "We want to protect you from everything, even us, if it ever comes down to it."

"For taking pleasure without asking us and for not

telling us about the calls, you are going to be punished. A very special punishment."

Oh, no, she didn't like the sound of that. It was hard keeping her head up, but she tried. The men sauntered across the room, but she couldn't see what they were getting. Tired of tilting her head to watch them, she finally let it drop. She saw their feet when they walked on either side of her before they disappeared behind her. She was totally open to whatever they wanted to do to her.

"Don't forget we want to hear your pleasure, subbie. Moans, groans, screams, cries. Everything," Ry said.

"First things first," Jed said. He touched her butt plug, and she automatically tightened around it, then she forced herself to relax.

Jed pulled the plug from her ass, and Katie breathed a sigh of relief. That damn thing had teased her all day, but her relief only lasted a minute before another plug was inserted. At least it wasn't as big as the last one.

"And now we will start," Ry said.

The plug in her ass began to vibrate. Katie jerked and let out a small cry of surprise. Her eyes widened as Jed's head slid under her. Because of the way she was positioned in the kneeling stockade, there was room between the floor and her chest for his big body.

"Pretty nipples," he said before covering one breast with his mouth.

She puffed out a breath as Jed sucked on her nipples, making them hard little peaks. Then a sharp, quick pain had her sucking in her breath.

He'd put on a set of tweezer clamps connected by a chain, and she knew what that meant. He and Ry were going to pull the chain while they tormented her. Tingles of excitement slid up her spine. But wait. There was another chain and clamp.

"You will ask us for permission to come," Ry said, his fingers spreading her pussy lips apart. He lifted the other clamp and attached it to her clit.

"And you will not come until we give you permission."

She sucked in a breath as the clamp closed over her clit. "Yes, Sirs."

Katie didn't know how much time had passed. At first, she didn't think her punishment was going to be that bad. Ry and Jed massaged her back and her front. It wasn't until they started pulling the chain, causing a streak of fire between her nipples and clit, that she realized she was in for a long session.

The vibrating plug in her ass was kept on low, just enough to drive her insane. After they pulled off the nipple and clit clamps, the men took turns swatting her ass with their hands. Then they slid a small vibrator in her pussy and began fucking her with it.

"Oh, God, please let me come, Sirs." How many times had she begged? She'd lost count. Each time their answer was the same. No. Her pussy clamped down with each stroke of the vibrator, and she wasn't sure how much longer she could hold on. The vibrations and feeling so full from the two toys had her on edge.

"Not yet, Kitty Kat." Jed stroked her spine in a soothing motion as the two vibrators were turned off.

She puffed out a breath in relief. The one in her pussy was removed, then the one from her ass. Both her core and ass twitched after being filled for so long.

"Punishment over," Ry said as he unfastened the cuffs on her legs. He then gripped her around the waist, slightly lifting her.

Jed removed the cuffs on her wrists. "Support yourself for a minute."

She nodded and kept her weight on her elbows. Jed swept the kneeling stock out from beneath her.

"Relax, sweetheart. I'll lower you to the floor," Ry said.

Trusting he wouldn't let her fall, Katie let her arms go limp. Ry guided her onto the mat, and Jed knelt near her head.

Jed rubbed her arms and elbows while Ry massaged her legs.

"That feels so good." Their firm massage worked the kinks out of her legs and arms from being restrained. Their hands against her skin also inflamed her passion.

"Can you stand up now?" Jed asked.

"I think so, Sir."

Together, the men got her into a sitting position, then helped her to her feet. She swayed, and Jed slid behind her, his chest against her back.

"Table." They said it together.

Jed lifted her into his arms and carried her over to the bondage table. He placed her on her feet next to the table. This time she didn't wobble.

"Now, little one, we're both going to fuck you."

Excitement flowed through her veins, but at the same time, she wasn't sure she'd be able to handle it. Hell, the small vibrator in her pussy and the vibe in her ass had filled her completely. What would it be like with both of their large cocks? She shivered.

"You're ready for this, Katie." Ry cupped her cheek with his palm.

She nodded. They would be gentle with her, and if she told them to stop, they would. Jed adjusted the bondage table so the top part was at an incline. Then he hopped up onto it and leaned back, his cock hard and ready.

"Climb up and over Jed," Ry said.

Katie looked from Ry and back to Jed. How the heck was she going to do that? Before she could ask, Ry grasped her by the waist and lifted.

"Climb on the table and kneel next to Jed," Ry said.

She did as he instructed.

Ry crowded behind her and placed his hands on her waist. "Now, raise one knee up and swing over Jed's groin. I'll help you."

Her teeth drew her lower lip into her mouth as she placed her hands on Jed's shoulders and swung her leg over him. With Ry's strong grip on her waist, she was able to swing around much easier than if she'd done it on her own. She straddled Jed.

Jed's cock brushed her ass, and her back stiffened. How were they going to do this?

"Easy, Kitty Kat." Jed slid one hand to her hip, and she lowered her head until she was staring at Jed's face. His forehead was scrunched up in concentration.

"Stay right there, sweetheart." Ry's hands tightened on her waist.

Jed's free hand skimmed over her inner thighs. Her core tightened. His touch was so soft, so erotic.

"Now slide down onto my dick."

With both Ry and Jed helping her, she lowered herself onto Jed's hard cock. She let out a breath as the head slipped into her wet pussy. A moan of pleasure escaped her lips as he continued to fill her inch by inch.

"That's it, baby," Ry said, rubbing her back. "Now lean forward until your breasts are against Jed's chest."

Katie resisted collapsing against Jed's chest, her

breath coming in short pants. How much more could she take? This position made Jed's cock feel even bigger in her pussy. Her muscles clenched around him. She could feel every twitch of his dick.

"That's it, Kitty Kat." Jed's hands soothingly skimmed over her back and down to her ass. "Are you okay?"

"Yes, Sir," she whispered. Her core contracted around his erection. "Want to move." She shifted from side to side.

"Be still." Jed's command, along with the quick swat to her butt, made Katie's excitement levels raise. "Just so you're prepared, Ry is about to apply lube to your ass."

The cool lube made her shiver. Ry's fingers massaged her, and one finger penetrated her ass.

"That's it. Let me in," Ry crooned as he pushed another finger into her ass.

Katie's mouth dropped open; it was almost too much.

"I can feel your fingers, Ry," Jed said.

Jed's words made Katie's blood sing with apprehension and need.

Ry inserted a third finger.

"Ohhh." Katie started to rise on her knees. Nerve endings came alive under his touch.

"Are you okay?" Jed placed his hands on her shoulders, keeping her in place.

"It feels incredible." And it did. Ry's fingers slowly pushed into her ass. Her anticipation went up a notch. They'd talked about this when they first started preparing her for anal penetration. She told them she wanted her first time to be with both of them. How would it feel when he put his cock in there?

Jed massaged her shoulders.

Ry's fingers slipped out of her ass, and then the pressure of his cock nudged her opening.

Katie stiffened, and Jed slipped his hands to her waist.

"Jed, wait. She's so tight." Ry backed away.

"No." Katie whimpered. She wanted to take both of them.

"Shh, Kitty Kat." Jed slid his lips over her cheek.

"Easy, sweetheart." Ry placed a kiss on her shoulder. "Katie, onto your knees. Jed, hands on her ass."

"But…"

Ry slapped her ass cheek.

"Sorry, Sir." Slowly, she rose, enjoying the friction from Jed's dick teasing the inside of her pussy.

"Stop right there," Ry ordered.

Jed's cock rested right against her opening.

"Katie, Jed is going to pull your ass cheeks apart. I want you to relax as much as possible. Go ahead, Jed."

Jed's fingers spread her ass cheeks, and Katie closed her eyes.

"Relax," Ry said.

"I'm trying." She worked on keeping herself as relaxed as possible. She tried to think of it as a really big butt plug; she didn't mind those.

Ry's cock pushed against her ass, and she fought against stiffening.

"Let him in, Kitty Kat," Jed said, pulling her attention back to him.

"Too big," she whispered, her eyes closing. Her ass was burning as Ry pushed his cock into her ass.

"No, he's not." Jed released her ass cheeks and pushed her hair away from her face. "Look at me, Kitty Kat."

She opened her eyes and focused on Jed's face. His eyes were bright with desire, his breathing ragged.

"Breathe in and out. That's it. Concentrate on me."

Ry paused for a second and nudged again against her tight ring. More and more pressure… Her mouth fell open, and she cried out when the head of Ry's cock breached her opening. "Oh, God." The burning sensation changed to pure pleasure.

Ry pushed farther into her ass, and she let out a soft cry.

"Kitty Kat?"

"I'm okay." She forced the words through her lips.

Ry's lips caressed a line up her spine as he shifted inside her full ass. "Now, slowly lower yourself onto Jed's cock, Katie."

Her mouth was open, and her breath was coming in short pants. Focusing her gaze on Jed's features, she started to lower herself. Oh, dear God. How did one describe the stretching, the pleasure flowing through her body? Her clit throbbed in time with her pounding heart.

"Fuck," Jed swore.

"Sir?" Katie hesitated.

"Don't stop. Please, Kitty Kat."

Inch by inch, Jed slipped into her pussy. The pressure from Ry's cock in her ass made her tighten her muscles around him. She sank down on the last few inches of Jed's cock and let out a moan.

"I can feel you both. So damn big." She laid her forehead against Jed's sweaty shoulder.

Their harsh breathing filled the room. "Full," she whispered. "So full." And she was. She was trapped between the two of them, and she wasn't sure she'd survive.

"You did so well, sweetheart," Ry said, kissing his way down her spine.

"Are you ready?" Jed asked.

Katie lifted her head and stared into his blue eyes. "Ready for what, Sir?"

Jed grinned, and Ry laughed. "For us to fuck you."

"I won't survive."

"Yes, you will." With those words, Jed placed his hands on her hips and lifted her.

His cock drew out, making her pussy tingle. He guided her back down, and Ry slid his cock almost out of her ass. Her core tightened around Jed, her ass clenching around Ry. The fullness would ease for a moment, and then it would come back with pure pleasure. The burning in her ass disappeared as every nerve ending in her body came alive with elation.

Every time Ry thrust into her ass, her pussy would tighten, then when Jed would push into her pussy, her ass clamped down, and her clit throbbed.

"Christ, Ry, I can feel your cock as you push into her," Jed said, his breath brushing against her sensitive skin.

"Same for me. And her ass is grabbing onto my dick."

"I'm not going to last long," Jed said.

"Katie?" Ry asked.

"Yes, Sir." Hell, she couldn't even figure out how she could speak. Pleasure spiked through her veins.

"How close are you?"

"Very." And she was. Without her knowing it, her climax was right on the edge.

"Good. You may come at will, subbie." Ry kissed the back of her neck. "Ready, Jed?"

"Fuck, yeah."

Katie moaned. Pure satisfaction hit her blood stream as both men thrust in and slid out. Faster and harder. Small flutters started in her core, moving to her stomach, and soon spreading throughout her entire being. She was going to come. She threw her head back, letting out a scream as her pussy and ass clamped down. She ground her clit against Jed's groin.

"Damn, Kitty Kat," Jed groaned.

"Come for us, subbie. Don't hold back, let us hear you."

She didn't know how, but the men seemed to fuck her even faster. Katie went with the flow. Her clit pulsed in time with their thrusts. Her breath caught in her throat as new tremors made their way from her ass, to her pussy, to her clit, and finally through her system. Her body didn't even feel like it was her own anymore. She screamed as another climax began ripping through her.

Jed slammed into her pussy and held still as he came, her pussy milking his cock.

"I can feel your release, Jed," Ry said, still pumping in and out of her ass. "So fucking tight."

Jed tilted her head up and captured her lips with his.

She cried out against Jed's mouth as Ry thrust into her ass, and he shouted out his release. Her ass tightened around his cock and her pussy around Jed's shaft.

"God, Katie," Ry said, his body hard and sweaty against her back. "You are so fucking beautiful."

Jed released her lips so she could breathe again.

"So full," she whispered. She was so happy, snuggling between the two men, her body lax from their love making.

They lay there for several minutes before Ry lifted himself off Katie. She whimpered, another mini-orgasm flowing through her when he pulled his cock out.

"Okay?" Ry asked.

Her body shook, and Jed let out a groan. "She's coming again."

"You set me off again when you pulled out of my ass," she told Ry.

"Shower time," Jed said.

"I can't move." And she couldn't. She was boneless and sated.

"I think we can help with that." Ry lifted her off Jed's cock, then into his arms.

Katie moaned at the loss of Jed's cock but curled into Ry's embrace as he carried her into the bathroom.

This was going to be a wonderful weekend.

Chapter 17

On Monday, Katie found herself smiling for no reason at all. Okay, maybe there was a reason. Two of them. Ry and Jed. They'd had a wonderful weekend together and not just all sex, either. Saturday, they'd spent time curled up on the sofa watching movies, eating junk food, and just cuddling with each other.

Sunday, they'd taken the horses out for a ride on the ranch and cooked a late lunch before she went home.

Both Ry and Jed had taken care of her, making sure she wasn't too sore, but also making sure she was satisfied. As if she wouldn't be after their loving her. Her lips turned up in a smile. She couldn't wait until they pleasured her like that again.

Sitting down at her desk, she turned on her computer and started checking her email. Nothing urgent, so she began working on the ranch accounts. When the doorbell rang at ten, she frowned. Who would be coming to the house?

Saving her work, she went to the front door and looked out the peep hole. What the hell? Her fingers shook as they curled around the knob. Part of her didn't want to open it, but she knew she had to. If she didn't, Walter and her father would never leave her alone. She twisted the knob and pulled the wooden door ajar.

"Hello, Katherine." Walter said, pushing his hand into

the pocket of his suit pants.

* * * *

"Sheriff," Josh said from the doorway of Ry's office.

Ry lifted his head from the nuisance reports from the weekend. Monday was already turning out to be very busy. After a quiet period, it now looked like the vandals were back again. Mainly broken windows and cars prowls.

"What's up?" He looked at his deputy.

"Mabel just got a call. Suspicious vehicle."

"Okay, go check it out." He went back to the mound of paperwork on his desk.

"I thought you might want, too, boss. It's in front of Miss Mazie's house."

Ry was on his feet as Josh finished his sentence. Snatching up his hat, Ry ran out to his SUV. His cell rang as he pulled out of the driveway. "McKade here."

"Get the hell out of this house."

That was Katie's voice. What the fuck? He floored the SUV. Had someone broken into her house?

"Now, Katherine—"

"Don't 'Katherine' me. Get out."

She knew the person. At least it wasn't a stranger.

"I want nothing to do with you, Walter. You or my father."

He concentrated on her voice. It was strained, but not afraid. Katie must have dialed his cell and set the phone down. Pushing the mute button, he got on his radio. "Betty, call Jed and get him over to Miss Mazie's house."

"Yes, Sheriff."

"You're coming back to New York City," the male voice said.

Fear gripped him so hard he couldn't breathe. Was he going to lose her again?

"Like hell I am."

Ry grinned. The pressure in his chest lessened. Good, Katie wasn't going to take any of this man's crap.

"What the hell is going on in here?"

Jed. Ry frowned. How had Jed gotten there so quickly? It had been maybe a minute or two since he told Betty to call him.

"Jed." The relief in Katie's voice was heartwarming to Ry. The tension in his spine eased.

"This has nothing to do with you," Walter said.

"Get out, Walter, and don't come back."

"Oh, I'll be back."

There was quiet for a minute or two. Then a door slammed.

"Okay, Kitty Kat?" Jed asked.

Ry pulled up to the house just as a white Mercedes pulled away from the house. Walter, he hoped. He quickly noted the license plate, called in to Betty that he was on scene, and then jogged up the walk.

Everything looked all right inside Miss Mazie's house. Nothing seemed out of place, so there was no fight or anything like that. Katie was standing quietly in Jed's arms.

"Okay?" Ry asked.

Katie's head lifted, and she held a hand out to him.

Ry took the offered hand, and they pulled him into their embrace. His heart stuttered before resuming its normal beat. She'd called him. She trusted him to help her, but he did wonder how she got also got a hold of Jed so fast. His arms tightened around her. As soon as they had everything sorted out, he'd follow up to make sure Walter had left town. But for right now, there was no place he'd rather be than here with his lovers, holding them.

How long they stood there, he didn't know and didn't care. This was for Katie, for Jed, and for himself.

When they broke apart, Ry saw her cell on the side table. He picked it up and ended the call. "What happened?"

"I think we better sit down. This might take some time." Katie blew out a breath.

Ry called in and let them know that everything was good, and he was going to take a very early lunch.

"Please, sit on the sofa," Katie said, heading for the nearby chair.

"With us," Jed said, taking her hand and guiding her to the sofa between them. "Thank you for calling me."

So that's how Jed had gotten here so quickly.

"And me." Ry took her left hand and squeezed.

"I was a little short with you, Jed."

Jed chuckled. "Short but I liked hearing the words 'Need you, now' from those lips." He glanced up at Ry. "How did she call you?"

"I dialed his number on my cell and left it on the table."

"Which I appreciate." Ry still wanted to go after that man and beat the crap out of him, but he'd wait.

"Who was the guy?" Jed asked.

"Walter, my ex-boyfriend."

"And he's here because?" Ry asked even though he knew the answer. Jed needed to be aware.

"Because he and my father cannot accept reality. I'm not going back to New York City."

When she said the words, the constriction in Ry's chest loosened.

"Do you want to tell us why he thinks you would?" Jed asked.

"Because he thinks he's God's gift to women."

Laughter filled the room, and Katie's hand relaxed in his.

"I know my father isn't anyone's favorite topic, but I think it's time you understood why I did what I did when I was eighteen."

"I know we've discussed it a little bit; you said we didn't scare you off, so I've always assumed it had something to do with your father," Jed said.

"I was scared, yes, but not of the two of you. Maybe of the lifestyle you led, but never of you as men." She squeezed each of their hands. "I was chasing a dream. You both know my father left my mother when I was eight. Mom did her best to raise me. When she died, Randall couldn't be bothered with me. Gran raised me from the time I was fourteen."

Ry stiffened, and Jed's fingers tightened around hers. "Katie," Ry started.

"Let me get this out, Ry. Please." She stared at him until he nodded.

Having Walter show up on her doorstep had her determined not to lose the two men she loved. Calling them had been an automatic response.

"Randall approached me a few days before my eighteenth birthday. He offered me a job in New York City and everything. I thought maybe he was ready to be a father to me." She pushed back the disappointment. "He came back the day after my eighteenth birthday, right after you two had left, with Peggy Morris in tow."

Both men swore, and Katie smiled sadly.

"I told you about what she had said. My father pushed me into making a decision right then and there. He gave an ultimatum—either I go with him, or I become a play toy for the two of you." She let out a sigh. "I was confused. I so wanted a relationship with my father. But he never really cared about me, only what he thought he could get from me."

"And what did he want?" Jed asked.

"Someone who could take suspicion away from him and Walter." She shook her head. "I guess I wasn't really paying attention. I missed Felton's Creek, and I missed both of you. Even if I didn't realize it at the time."

"Did he hurt you?" Ry's voice was low, and she squeezed his hand.

"No. He never touched me."

"There are other ways to hurt, Kitty Kat," Jed said.

"I know." She smiled. Her fear of not being enough of a woman for the two of them was fading. "Anyway, I went with him. About a three years ago, Randall introduced me to Walter. We went out, but I knew he wasn't right for me. I liked him, but there was no spark. My father kept inviting Walter to events he insisted I be at. Things like that." Looking back now, she realized she hadn't put up much of a fight, either, and that had been her mistake. "After a while, I just didn't care enough to argue with Walter or my father. About a year after I started working for Randall's company, I began to notice things."

"Right, you said you worked at another company until your father bought it out," Jed commented.

"Like what?" Ry asked.

"Discrepancies in some of the accounts I managed. Small but they were still there. I talked with my boss, who talked to his boss, and I was told they were aware of them and not to worry about them."

"But that wasn't the end of it," Jed said.

"Nope. They kept getting bigger and bolder, so I did

some backtracking on my own."

"That was dangerous." Ry lifted her hand and kissed her knuckles.

"I didn't think about it. I was just doing the job I was hired for. When I found out what was going on and who it traced back to, I knew what I had to do." She took a deep breath. "I knew it was time to come home."

"What did you do, Kitty Kat?"

"I had planned on confronting my father and Walter about my findings, but…" Her anger at her father and Walter returned as she remembered the night she confronted them. Anger, disappointment, and the fear of her own wants and needs had clashed that last night in her father's place. "God, sometimes I wish I could forget certain things."

The guys' reactions were instantaneous. Their hands left hers, and they put their arms around her shoulders and on her waist, giving her as much comfort and support as they could with the way they were sitting.

"I'd gone to my father's apartment. I had a key and let myself in." She could still hear the odd noises coming from the back of the apartment. "At first, I thought there was no one home until I heard a cry from the back bedroom. I followed the noise and found my father and Walter."

"Oh, hell, they were fucking each other," Ry said.

"If only," she whispered. "They had a prostitute, and they were whipping her."

Both men stiffened, and Katie tilted her head back.

"Not like you two, nothing like you do. This wasn't for her pleasure but theirs. I could tell the difference from being at the clubs."

"What did you do?" Jed asked.

"I screamed, and I scared the shit out of everyone. I

marched up to the poor woman, helped her out of the X frame they had her tied to, and took her into the bathroom." She remembered the poor woman flinching as she cleaned her up. "She had several cuts on her back from the whip. Her name was Judy. I talked with her as I cleaned her up and bandaged her wounds. I found out she had been a student but had fallen in with the wrong crowd and was now beholden to some pimp."

Her anger rose. Her father was a predator. He walked out on her as a child, then came back and fed her lines of what she wanted to hear. Her father was sadist. He got off on other people's pain. No more. She was in control of her life.

"I left her in the bathroom with some of my old sweats and a T-shirt, told her to dress, and not to worry. Then I went out and faced my father and Walter."

"That could not have been fun," Ry said.

"Hell, those two deserved each other. My father was furious, but Walter just looked guilty. I told my father I was taking Judy with me when I left. Randall started to try to explain, but I told him I didn't want to hear his lies. He was a monster and a hypocrite. And I quit. Then I marched back and got Judy, and we left."

"And they just let you?"

"I think they were both in shock. My father because I actually told him off, and Walter out of guilt."

"What did you do with Judy?" Jed asked.

"We went to my apartment. I called Dr. Pam, and she came over. After a few hours, she had a place for Judy to stay where she'd be safe. Pam started counseling Judy the next day."

"What about you?" Ry asked.

"Me? I packed up my apartment, arranged for my stuff

to be shipped here, got in my car, and came home." She kissed Ry's jaw and then Jed's. "It was time. I was tired of the City, of my father and Walter, but I also missed Gran." The fluttering in her stomach encouraged her to continue. "And I missed both of you. I missed your voices, your strength, and your attention."

The room went silent, and Katie peeked at the men from beneath her lashes. The surprise and love on their faces caused the last of the tension to drain out of her body.

"What you saw didn't color your views of us and our lifestyle?" Jed asked.

"No. There was nothing safe and sane about what my father and Walter were doing. What we do is safe, sane, and consensual."

"We wouldn't have it any other way," Ry said.

"The city was just a place to live, and I missed home. Felton's Creek is home. Gran is home. You are both home. I let my father convince me what I would have with you was nothing but violence and shame. But he was the one with the violence and shame issues, not me." She snuggled closer to the men. "He made me doubt my feelings for both of you and doubt myself. But you've shown me real love. I'm sorry it took me so long to figure things out. I will never doubt us or what we have together. I don't."

"Never," both men whispered.

Chapter 18

Saturday morning, the sun was shining and not a cloud in the sky. This weekend was the annual Felton's Creek Celebration. Ry finished setting up the sheriff's office booth, then went to help Jed unload the horses from the trailer.

There was everything from booths selling homemade crafts and foods, to Jed with pony rides for the kids, to small carnival rides. It was a chance for the entire town to be out and celebrating.

Katie was going to be helping Miss Mazie at her tea booth, and then later, the three of them would find a spot on the grass to watch the fireworks. After what she told them the other night about her father and Walter whipping the young lady, Ry was still amazed how she reacted to him and Jed.

Her father and Walter only wanted to cause pain and degradation, whereas Ry and Jed wanted to give her pleasure, taking her to the next level of satisfaction and sexual release. Her submission was a gift, one Ry would honor for the rest of his life.

"Hey, Jed, I've been thinking," Ry said as he helped with the horses.

"That's dangerous."

"Watch yourself, sub." Ry grinned, and Jed just laughed. "When do we want to discuss making things permanent with Katie?"

Jed stopped in his tracks and stared at Ry. "You want

to talk about that now?"

Ry nodded. He'd been toying with the idea in his head for a while, and after she told them about her father and ex, he wanted nothing more than to find a way to keep her in their lives. "It's time. We're not getting any younger."

"How do you think we should handle this?" Jed moved the horse into the temporary stable.

"We have to ask her first."

"I know that." Jed shut the stall door and leaned against it.

"I've been thinking about that, and I'm hoping you'll agree. But there's another issue."

"And that is?"

Ry frowned. Usually, Jed was the one to jump into things without thinking. "We'll be coming out to the whole town."

"I think the town knows about us. We don't flaunt our relationship with Katie and our parents never hid their relationship with each other."

"No, they didn't." Ry fondly remembered going out with his family and being proud of having two dads and a special mother who kept him and Jed in line.

"Your parents were married," Jed said, leading the last horse into the temporary stabling. "But my dad never married your mom, nor did he collar her."

He rubbed the back of his neck. What he was suggesting wasn't necessarily welcomed in most places. "Alternative lifestyle" was the current politically correct term. "True, but are you telling me you'd be willing to play a third without being committed to Katie and me?"

"I am committed." Jed marched over to him. "But legally, only one of us can marry her."

"True. Tell me how you feel about this." Ry was

putting a lot on the line here, but he wasn't willing to lose Katie or Jed. He'd compromise if needed. "Let's talk to Katie and get her thoughts. If she agrees, we can legally have all our last names hyphenated. It will show how committed we are. We can also do a handfasting ceremony after whomever Katie chooses for a legal marriage."

Ry studied Jed's face, his nerves stretched taut when Jed didn't respond. But his features were bland, containing no anger or fear. Maybe he was receptive to this.

"And then we can have a collaring ceremony with her," Ry continued. "We can both collar her and the three of us wear rings."

Jed's eyes widened, and Ry blew out a breath.

A grin broke out over Jed's face. "We need to tread carefully with Katie on this. But I like it."

"I agree, but I love her, and it's time."

"Agreed. I love her and you, you big lug." Jed pulled him into a hug, and Ry returned it.

"I love you, too, sub. So let me tell you what I found in Monroe. Since the catalog items didn't work out. Actually, we can run to Monroe right now, pick it up, and be back before the celebration starts."

"Let's go."

* * * *

"Enjoy your tea," Katie said as she handed the bag over to the older woman.

"Oh, I will."

Katie put the money in the register and sighed. It had been busy most of the day at Gran's booth. The Felton's Creek Celebration always brought a lot of people in. While she had dinner each night this week with Ry and Jed, she'd only seen them in passing today.

Jed had a small ring set up for pony rides, and Ry

would roam around while leaving his deputy with the SUV, looking absolutely delicious in his uniform.

"Why don't you take a break?" Gran asked.

"Are you sure?"

"Yeah, go." She patted Katie on the shoulder. "Go find your men."

Katie grinned and kissed Gran's cheek before leaving the booth. Gran was such a wonderful woman.

She was halfway to the riding ring when little Tommy Miller ran into her, his blond hair sticking out and his shirt dusty.

"Oops, sorry, Miss Katie."

"It's okay." After helping Tommy gain his footing, she straightened to see her father and Walter standing in front of her. Her stomach dropped. She'd hoped they left town for good. "What do you want?"

"We need to talk," her father said.

Tommy wrapped himself around her legs. Katie knelt. "Tommy, go to the riding ring, right now," she whispered in the boy's ear. "Let Jed know I sent you. Nowhere else, understand?"

Tommy nodded, let go of her legs, and took off running. She could only hope he'd tell Jed what he saw.

Chapter 19

"Sheriff, sheriff."

Ry turned from the horse ring at the sound of the young voice. Tommy Miller came running up to him out of breath. "Easy, Tommy." He knelt and took the small boy by the shoulders. "Where's the fire?" It was a question he always asked when kids were like this.

"Miss Katie sent me to get Mr. Jed," he panted. "There are two scary men with her."

Ry jerked his head up, trying to see to Miss Mazie's booth, but he couldn't. "Good job, Tommy." He stood. "Jed, we've got a problem."

Jed hopped the fence and marched over to him. "What's up?"

"Katie's in trouble." He looked down at Tommy. "Where was she, Tommy?"

"Over there." He waved his hand in the direction of the tea booth.

"Thanks, buddy." Ry smiled.

"Go get your ride." Jed turned Tommy toward the ring and gave him a pat on the head.

Together, they sprinted in the direction Tommy had waved. It didn't take a genius to guess that her father and the ex were here and harassing Katie. Well, it was time to show them a united front. It didn't take them long to find her. Katie was standing with her feet apart, her hands on her hips as she gave the two men standing in front of her hell.

"What's going on, sweetheart?" Ry asked as he and Jed encircled her. His arm went around her waist, and Jed's went right above his. Ry brushed his lips against her right temple.

Jed did the same on her left. "Okay, Kitty Kat?"

"Better," she whispered, melting into their embrace.

The older man in front of Katie made a noise, and Ry looked him over: his hair gray, his pinched lips, and the lines creasing the man's forehead. Katie's father. The man standing next to him was younger, and his expression of distaste made Ry want to laugh. The ex was less of a threat.

"I told you to leave," Katie said, steel running through her voice.

Ry was proud of her. She wasn't going to take any crap from these two.

"Not until you agree to come back."

Ry squeezed Katie's waist, and Jed did the same.

"I've already told you, Father. I'm not coming back."

"Maybe this will change your mind." Ry didn't like the gleam that came into her father's eyes. The man was up to something. "You come back, and I won't expose these two to the entire town."

Ry started to remove his arm from Katie's waist, but she wrapped hers around his waist, tightening it to let him know she supported him.

Katie lifted her chin and stared at her father. "First off, I don't know what you're talking about. I'm happy, and I don't plan on leaving Felton's Creek."

"How the hell can you be happy in this little hick town?" the younger man asked.

Katie took a sharp breath. "It's not a hick town, and you stay out of this, Walter."

"It comes down to choices, Katherine. Either come

back with Walter and me or I expose these two to the entire town."

"Expose what?" She shook her head.

"How about I tell everyone here how these two have been with my daughter, together, doing unspeakable things to her, against her will?"

Ry and Jed took a step forward, and Katie latched onto their belts. Ry glanced down at her, but she was staring at the two men. Her grip on their belts didn't ease up.

The carnival music, ringing bells, and the voices from the celebration were more prominent at Katie's silence. Damn. He was the one who told her they didn't flaunt their relationship in front of the town. But he wasn't going to keep it a secret, either. Not when they decided it was time to take the next step.

He glanced over at Jed, who was staring at him. Jed nodded. They were in agreement. It didn't matter who knew about them. They weren't giving Katie up without a fight.

"Katie."

"No, Ry." Her voice was low and tight. "You are such a hypocrite, Father. Have you conveniently forgotten what I walked in on before I left?"

Her father's gaze turned freezing cold. He held up his hand. "Excuse me, everyone." His voice was loud enough to garner attention.

Katie's chin dropped to her chest, and Ry's heart contracted.

"Is there a problem?" Mayor Thompson asked, walking up to them.

It was do-or-die time. Ry stiffened his spine.

"Yes, these two men won't leave my daughter alone so we can talk."

"You say you're Katie's father?" Mayor Thompson asked.

"Yes, that scum is." Gran's voice was strong and clear. All eyes turned toward Miss Mazie, who held two young teenagers by the ears. More people gathered around the group. "I saw these two boys talking with Randall behind my booth, and I just happened to overhear the conversation. Tell them, boys."

The boys looked down at their feet, scuffing their toes in the grass. "We're the ones who keyed the car, broke the windows, and some of the other stuff," one said.

"They said to just scare her, but they never paid us," the other said, pointing at Katie's father and Walter.

"What about the attempted robberies?" Ry asked.

"We didn't try to rob anyone. I swear, Sheriff. We would never do that." The one boy looked up at him, and Ry saw the truth in his eyes.

The boys' parents had joined the group, and both sets glared at their children. The fathers stepped forward and took an arm of each son. "We'll take care of this, Sheriff."

"Bring them by the office. I'm sure we can work something out with the judge for community service for the entire summer to pay for the damages." But that still didn't explain the couple of robberies they'd had.

The boys groaned.

The older teen glanced from Ry to Katie's father. "He hired two ex-cons who live in Monroe to do the robberies, Sheriff. They bragged to us about it, but we refused to help."

Ry's anger built. It could have been much worse than it was. Ry nodded, then turned his attention back to Katie's father.

Randall's gaze was still hard and defiant. "It's their

word against ours." A sinister grin spread over her father's lips, and Ry had a bad feeling.

Katie's head was still bowed.

"These two men standing here are anything but upstanding citizens. I don't know about the state laws around here, but they are perverts. They are not normal. They prefer having sex together and share a woman."

"We've done nothing wrong," Ry whispered in her ear.

"Damn right." Her head came up.

"Katie?" the mayor looked at her, then to Ry and Jed.

"Mayor." Her voice was soft, hesitant. She glanced up at Jed and then Ry. She cleared her throat. "I love Ry McKade and Jed Malloy."

Jed jerked, and Ry did the same. She loved them? Why hadn't she told them?

"These two men make me happy, and if Felton's Creek residents can't understand and accept it, then it's the town's problem."

Ry let out a breath. Okay, this wasn't the way he wanted this to go down, but the hell with it. He'd resign as sheriff if need be. He wasn't giving up Katie or Jed.

The mayor stared at the three of them before turning his attention to Katie's father. "I don't give a damn who you are," the mayor said. "You are a stranger to this town and so is this fellow." The mayor waved his hand at both of them. "Ryland and Jedidiah are honorable, decent citizens of this town. Ryland is our sheriff, and he will be for a long time. Jedidiah donates his time and horses so the kids know how to ride and learn about them. As for Katie…"

The mayor glanced at her. "She is a beautiful young woman, a brilliant accountant. What they do in their private life is their business. I will stand behind them. Who'll join me?" The major stepped next to Ry.

All around the trio, the crowd shifted. Ry held his breath. The mayor supported them, but did anyone one else? Katie glanced around. Most of the town stood behind them. Ry noted a several people walked away, and it didn't bother him.

"There's your answer, Father. It's time to leave."

"They need to answer for the vandalism to Katie's car," Ry said.

"No charges, Ry." Katie tilted her head to the side and went up on her toes. "They've got more problems than just vandalism."

"Get out," someone yelled.

"Leave our town," another voice added.

"We don't need trash like you around," yet another called out.

All of it came from the people surrounding them.

"You will regret this," Randall said.

"That sounded like a threat." Jed glared at the man.

"No, Father, I will never regret this. I regret I never saw you for the shallow, selfish, cruel man you were until a few months ago. And you, Walter, you're just my father's puppet. Oh, and by the way, the Feds should be raiding the company any time now."

Her father's eyes widened. "What did you do?"

Walter whimpered.

"Let them know about the books being off. I'm not as stupid as you think, Randall. Did you really think I'd miss the fact that you are stealing from your employees' retirement funds?" She tilted her chin up. "Go away."

"Leave and never come back," Jed said.

"I couldn't have said it better," Ry added.

Without another word, the two men turned and all but ran to their car.

The crowd let out a cheer.

"Now let's get this celebration back to being fun," the mayor announced.

Katie let out a laugh, and Ry knew they were going to be okay.

* * * *

Later that night, just as it was turning dark, Katie sat between Ry and Jed on a blanket underneath one of the oak trees. The fireworks would start soon. Katie glanced at the two men. They really hadn't talked about what had happened earlier. She didn't want to spoil their evening, but they needed to discuss it.

"Ry, Jed—"

Her grandmother meandered up to them.

Both men started to rise, but Gran waved them to stay seated. "Everything okay now?" she asked.

"I think I'm still in shock," Jed said.

"I don't know why." Gran put her hands on her hips, and Katie smiled.

"I'm with Jed," Ry said.

"You two boys should know by now almost the entire town would support you. Heck, everyone knew about your parents, and no one cared. What you do in your private life is your business and no one else's. But you had better take care of my Katie, or you'll have to answer to me."

Both men nodded before Gran grinned at her. "I won't expect to see you until tomorrow at the booth." And she ambled off.

Ry and Jed both let out a laugh, and Katie grinned. Gran was something else. But now, she needed to talk with the guys. She'd blurted out she loved them in front of the whole town without telling them first.

Katie rose to her knees and faced the two men. "We need to talk about today." Nerves had her twisting her fingers together.

Jed groaned, and Ry shook his head. Both men reached over, untangled her twined fingers, and each took a hand, holding it lightly.

"Do you really love us?" Jed asked.

"Yes," she whispered. "I think I've loved you since I was a teen." The pressure in her chest eased.

"I love you." Ry's fingers tightening on hers.

"And I love you," Jed said.

Her heart lightened. They loved her.

"And with that…" They rose to their knees in front of her. Oh, God, what were they doing?

"Katie Crane," Jed said. "I love you, and I want you to become my wife."

Her mouth dropped open as her gaze flicked from Ry to Jed, and back again, then back once more.

"Katie Crane," Ry said. "I love you more than life itself and would be honored if you'd become my wife."

"But…" She swallowed, her stomach rolling and dipping. "I can legally only marry one of you."

"We know." Reaching underneath the blanket they each pulled out a box.

Shivers of excitement slid through Katie's veins.

"This is for our wedding night," Ry said. He opened his box to show the beautiful collar, two strands of pearls connected with a black clasp at the back. The front had three silver, entwined hearts. "We picked it up this morning in Monroe."

"And these are for the ceremony," Jed said, opening his box, which held three gold rings.

Tears filled Katie's eyes.

"We've already talked to the pastor," Jed said.

"He agreed to marry the three of us. Only Ry's name will appear on the marriage license if that's okay with you. But we would like all of us to change all our last names to McCade-Malloy." Jed stared at her.

The tears slipped down her cheeks. "I love you both so much." She pulled her hands away from them only to throw her arms around their necks, hugging them tightly.

"Is that a yes?" Jed asked, amusement in his voice.

"Yes." She let out a laugh. "I'm proud to marry both of you and take your names. That's what the hyphen is for."

Katie's lips met Jed's and then Ry's as the fireworks went off overhead.

* * * *

Thank you for reading *Embracing Desire*. If you enjoyed this book, please consider leaving a review on Goodreads, or your favorite retailer. It is greatly appreciated. For new release information and news about Marie Tuhart, please join her **newsletter**.

There will be a *Wicked Sanctuary Christmas*, a novella, showing you the lives of the main characters in the series. This is a special book for readers to have. You will receive a free copy if you join my newsletter when the book releases at the end of September.

In 2025 I'll start releasing a new series *Fantasies Inc.*, a company that specializes in making fantasies come true. I'll also be releasing two cowboy books, and *One Weekend in Seattle* in a shared world series. Keep an eye out on my newsletter for updates.

Marie Tuhart lives in the beautiful Pacific Northwest with her two dogs, Tommy and Trina. Marie brings to life contemporary approachable alpha heroes and the spunky women who take them to task. Her high-heat, emotional books, many with BDSM elements, inviting the reader to slid the silky scarves between their fingers, fell the kiss of a flogger on their flesh in breathless anticipation of what or who will come next. Embrace the temptation and enjoy a happily ever after that's always about the heroine.

For up-to-date information about releases, please consider joining Marie's mailing list.

Check out Marie's website at: **https://www.marietuhart.com**

OTHER BOOKS BY MARIE TUHART

Claimed by the Sheikh
Billionaire's Cowboy's Conquest
More of You (Club Crave)
Reflections of you (Club Crave)
Bound to Love You (Club Crave)
Hot for You (Club Crave)
Tempt (Wicked Sanctuary Series)
Entice (Wicked Sanctuary Series)
Seduce (Wicked Sanctuary Series)
Ravish (Wicked Sanctuary Series)
Possess (Wicked Sanctuary Series)
Tantalize (Wicked Sanctuary Series)
Edged (Wicked Sanctuary Series)
Unmasked (Wicked Sanctuary Series)
Too Hot (Wicked Sanctuary Series)

Wicked Sanctuary Novellas:
Untamed
Power Play
Claiming Rose